MW01243055

i

The Irishmen

Don Allen

Cover, Don Allen Digital art 'Light House' 2023

ISBN: 979-8-9883175-3-1

eISBN: 979-8-9883175-2-4

Publisher: Don Allen

Also, by Don Allen

Sean Murphy Series
Satisfaction
Chaos
The Launderer
The Brotherhood
The Developer
Treasure

George Basdakis Series
Check for Junk
The Gurkha

Sam Goodwin Series
Dog Walker
The Irishmen

1 Introduction

The past eighteen months since my retirement from the Boston Police Department have been full of assaults, kidnappings, and terrorists, almost as if I had never retired. Carol, my wife, and I decided we needed a vacation.

I'm Samuel Goodwin, in my mid 50's and physically fit. For the past decade or more, I was assigned to the Boston Police Department's canine unit. Maxie is my eighty-pound, eleven years old, German Shepherd. When I left the force, she was too old for further police service. I petitioned the Mayor to be allowed to keep her. A few years earlier, Maxie and I were honored by Mayor Grace McGuire for our participation in a major drug bust. Since then, Mayor McGuire has been a Maxie supporter. No need to mention that the drug bust helped cement McGuire's reelection.

It's best if I go back a bit to paint a full picture. Fenk Ciziri, our neighbor across the street, is an Iraqi refugee, more specifically, an ethnic Yazidi. She works with the 'Boston Iraqi Refugee Center.' Early last year she recognized the ISIS commander who managed the 'Mosel Rape Hotel.' After reporting this to her supervisor, she was assaulted at home late one night, attempted murder by an intruder. Fortunately, Maxie was alerted by Muffy's barking, Fenk's poodle. We arrived in time to save her and capture her attacker. The attacker, a player in the latter part of this story, christened Maxie as 'the bitch from hell.' This encounter would eventually lead to our involvement with 'The Islamic Society of Boston.'

Concurrent with this excitement two noted BPD old-timers retired from the force. Danny O'Kaye and Jimmy Anderson, collectively known as 'Salt 'n Pepper.' Danny is a wiry little Irishman with pale

1

skin, blond hair, and blue eyes. In contrast, Jimmy, the 'Pepper' of this duo, is a former halfback. He's big, and, when provoked, mean. They opened the Salt 'n Pepper Detective Agency. Their first case was to find missing workers from restaurants in Boston's Chinatown. These workers were in the country illegally; the Tong had them smuggled in on Chinese cargo ships. Given their immigration status, the restaurant owners were reluctant to involve the authorities, thus the Restaurant Owners Association hired the newly formed Salt 'n Pepper Detective Agency to find the missing employees.

As it turned out the New York Tong was enticing workers to the Big Apple with better working conditions. Agreement between the two Tong chapters was reached; no more poaching and better work conditions in Boston.

These events brought Salt 'n Pepper and me together. While meeting with Lieutenant Doyle at *The Coffee Shope*, the BPD's unofficial headquarters, to discuss Fenk's case, Doyle introduced me to Danny. Danny offered me a job as a part-time PI. Part-time soon became full-time.

In the following months, we found those who had targeted Fenk, disrupted a people smuggling ring in the Southwest, and helped the FBI thwart a major terrorist attack ... poisoning NYC's water supply with fentanyl.

As I just said, my wife Carol and I felt a week's vacation was needed. Maxie was content to sit in the back seat with her head out the open window as we drove out of the city.

2 Maine

Our plan was to drive up the Maine coast revisiting places we enjoyed on past vacations. We invited Fenk to join us, but she was needed at the Refugee Center, being one of the few interpreters the Center had.

Our first stop was Billy's Bait Shop and Restaurant in Wells, a little less than a hundred-mile drive from our home in West Roxbury.

Wells, Maine, is a popular destination for Bostonians, not far, with nice beaches, good restaurants, and all the makings of a summer resort area. But with one downside, it was too close to Boston. The weekend vacation crowd filled the streets.

Billy's Bait Shop and Restaurant was on the beach at the end of the boardwalk. If truth be told, Billy's was okay, not the best, and the boardwalk was like other boardwalks up and down the East Coast. But the attraction for Carol and me, we had been going there for the past twenty, twenty-five years. It felt good to be there.

Years ago, I convinced the manager, Billy's daughter, that Maxie was a service dog. Since then, she was always welcomed with a bowl of water.

We had our usual two lobster rolls, each. Our final destination for the day was Boothbay Harbor, another seventy-five miles up the coast, a two-hour drive. Given that it was only one p.m., Carol thought we had time for a short stroll on the boardwalk. Not my first choice, but who am I?

Ten minutes away from the restaurant, and what happens? A teenage thug grabs a lady's purse shoving her to the ground. He takes off down the boardwalk, cutting into one of the alleys. I give chase. Maxie does her thing, and the youth is on the ground with a snarly dog on his back. It's not long before a cop from the beach arrives. The kid is yelling, "That dog attacked me!"

The officer looks at me; I point to the purse on the ground. "Do kids around here always carry purses?" I ask.

As I explained what had happened, the lady, the purse's owner, and her friend came down the alley yelling at the kid. Her friend, in a more measured tone, told the cop what had happened.

As he arrested the kid, the officer said, "I need everyone to come to the Police Station to make a statement." I convinced him I wasn't really needed. Maxie had inflicted no damage other than ripped pants. I gave him my contact information, collected Maxie, and we left.

Walking back to the car, Carol says with a grin, "Just can't avoid trouble, can you?"

Never one to leave well enough alone, I point out, "The walk on the boardwalk was your idea."

***

We had planned a leisurely trip up Rt. 1. A windshield tour of old haunts: Old Orchard Beach's beach arcade, which dates to the '30s; the Bush's summer home in Kennebunkport, and the discount store at LL Bean in Freeport. We would be stopping there on the trip home.

Due to our excursion on the Wells boardwalk, we lost an hour of travel time. We had reservations at Brown's Wharf Inn in Boothbay Harbor. Wanting to make up the time, we opted to take I-95. Less scenic but more direct.

Brown's Wharf Inn was on the peninsula across the small harbor from the town. Spruce Point Peninsula has undergone significant upgrades since Carol and I first visited the area three decades ago. Back in the day, the access road to the Inn was closed on November first in anticipation of heavy snowfall and not opened until April Fool's Day, an apt date. On the third of April 1987, Spruce Point Peninsula received three feet of snow.

Since our last visit to Boothbay Harbor, the development of the peninsula opened it up to year-round access. Brown's Wharf Inn had been expanded to include a marina, replacing the old farmhouse having the check-in counter, the lounge, dining room, and bar, and the quaint cabins with a three-floor motel. Carol insisted on reserving a room for sentimental reasons. I expect this will be our last visit.

As we drove into Boothbay Harbor, we were disappointed to see the Lobster Trap Restaurant had closed, replaced by a nondescript chain restaurant.

We checked into the motel, securing an end room on the second floor. The best I can say, it provided a good view of the harbor.

Deciding on an early dinner, we returned to the downtown area. Most of the small shops we remembered had closed; COVID casualties? The best we could find was an Italian restaurant, 'The Ports of Italy.' Have you ever tried lobster in marinara sauce? Don't! It's not natural.

Over breakfast the next morning, Carol suggested we move on. She had been doing some internet surfing and found what appeared to be what our memories wanted. The 'Bluebird Ocean Point Inn' was one peninsula over and in the township of Boothbay. This Inn was what Brown's Wharf Inn was at one time. It was remote, had cabins, and, most important, vacancies.

"What do you say, Sam? You check us out, and I'll call The Bluebird Ocean Point Inn."

We were packed and on the road by ten. It was only a fifteen-minute drive, but it took us back decades.

3 The Bluebird Ocean Point Inn

The Bluebird Ocean Point Inn looked like a nineteenth-century farmhouse. Three floors, the uppermost with dormers, and a giant wraparound porch. Although it looked like a nineteenth-century structure, it was built a century later and with modern amenities. The first floor had a dining room, a lounge, reception area, and a bar. Three guest rooms were on the second floor, and the owner, a retired Navy Chief Petty Officer, and his wife lived in the garret on the third.

Checking in I talked with the owner, "Any problem with dogs?"

"Not at all. If he tends to wander, I suggest a leash. If he gets lost in the woods, you'll never find him."

"Him? Maxie is insulted; he's a she. She's a retired police dog, as am I. Retired I mean, not a dog,' I said with a chuckle. "What got you out here, longtime local?"

"I'm Rick Dale, retired Navy; twenty-eight years. No, my wife and I are both from Kansas. We wanted a quiet place by the ocean and something to keep me busy, out from under her feet. We spend spring, summer, and fall here and winter in Boynton Beach where we have a double-wide in the Jima Bay retirement trailer park."

Our cabin was nestled in pine trees, two hundred yards from the ocean, separated from it by the perimeter road. There were three or four other cabins among the trees.

Carol settled in with her newest novel, a spy novel she was writing. She was close to finishing it and planned to submit it for editing when we returned home. Carol had seven books in print. She was becoming a noted author in the spy-mystery genera. Her last

6

three novels featured a Greek American with a defective moral compass. Carol's current work would be the fourth in the series.

The following morning as is my habit, I was up early and decided to take Maxie on a long walk along the perimeter road.

A small summer community, Ocean Point Beach, had been built at the peninsula's tip. Being early in the season, there were only a few people about. One was an elderly man out with his dog, a basset hound named Emelie. The two dogs did their normal sniffing, followed by mutual indifference.

"Too bad people can't do that," the man said. "People often have conflicts with those they don't understand."

"You must be new here; I know most folks hereabouts. I'm Bill Hardy, a retired journalist."

"Just a visitor for a few days. We're staying at The Bluebird Ocean Point Inn. I'm retired from the Boston police force, as is Maxie," I said as I pointed to her.

We walked for another half hour, me complaining about change, he mostly agreeing. I touched on my recent experience with the foiled fentanyl attack on NYC's water supply.

"As a city resident, that was a threat too close to home. I don't think you folks got the credit you deserved. I'm sorry to say our Mayor grabbed most of the headlines with my former colleagues supporting him."

"Your colleagues?" I asked.

"I was a reporter for the 'New York Times' for forty years. Your lamenting change takes a backseat to changes at the Gray Lady, mostly bad in my opinion."

As we started to part ways, he said, "I normally don't take to people so quickly, but for you, I'll make an exception. Would you and your significant other join my wife and me for drinks at five today?"

I accepted, and he provided directions to his cottage.

4 The Irishmen

Maxie and I were sitting on the cottage porch, me with my coffee and her with a bowl of kibbles. Carol finally appeared, saying, "It looked like the start of a beautiful summer day. What are we going to do?"

"Well, we can start with breakfast," I said. "The dining room is serving till nine. If we move along, we can make it."

We made it. I ordered a full breakfast, eggs, waffles, sausages, OJ, and coffee. Carol opted for a fruit dish with yogurt and tea. "That won't be enough to get you through the morning," I said, reviving a long-standing argument we've been having for years about a proper breakfast.

"That sounds like a discussion my wife and I have been having," said a voice from the next table. Looking over, the speaker was a smallish man with a well-trimmed black beard and an unruly head of hair. "I normally go for a full English breakfast," he said with a slight Irish lilt. His 'wife' was a large man looking like 'Mr. Clean' with wire-rim glasses. "I'm Jimmy McKee, and my wife is Billie Steele."

Not wanting to be rude to fellow vacationers, we engaged in a little small talk. The little guy said they were from Ballygawly, a small town in County Tyrone, Northern Ireland. They were visiting New England, tracing one of his wife's relatives exiled to the colonies by the Crown.

"That sounds like an interesting story," said Carol. "Let's move out onto the porch with our coffee or tea as one prefers, and you can fill us in on the details."

Shoot me, I'm thinking; Carol is looking for new material for a future novel. I have no interest, but being a supportive husband, I tag along.

"Seamus Twomey," the little guy picks up after we relocate, "was caught up in the 1680 protests against the Church of England. He was convicted of treason and faced either a noose or transportation to the colonies as an indentured servant. Choosing the latter and upon arrival in Boston, his contract was sold to a fishing fleet owner. He spent the next several years working as a virtual slave on a Gloucester fishing schooner. When set free, his only means of making a living was fishing. He moved up the coast and, working with other freed servants, made a living in the cod trade. He supposedly died in the early 1700s and was buried hereabouts."

After collecting a bit more background material, Carol gracefully extracts us from the two noting the time and saying we had an appointment with a realtor later in the morning.

"Oh, you are looking to buy a summer place," says Jimmy. "There are some nice cottages on Ocean Point Beach. We have a friend living there."

Returning to our cottage, "Looking to write a seventeenth-century thriller now? It will be a challenge to write your Greek American hero into that story," I said with a chuckle.

***

We arrived at the Hardy's cottage at five, on time. Bill was trimming the rose bushes, collecting blooms to take inside. As he welcomes us, he tells me to let Maxie out; she'll be fine. And goes on, "Trixie, my wife likes fresh flowers in the house. I try to get her some every day or so."

As we enter the living room, Bill introduces us to Trixie, a lady in her 60s in a wheelchair. "She was injured several years ago while visiting family in Ireland. Fell down some stairs and broke her back."

"Don't mind Bill now," Trixie says in a thick Irish brogue. "Other than these wheels, I'm as able as the next person. Where is Maxie? Bill has been telling me about her and your adventures."

Over drinks, scotch 'n water for me, I revisit my fentanyl story and go into some depth about the Islamic Society.

"I think we have something like that in New York," Bill says.

"You do. They provided the men who placed the fentanyl in the tunnel. There are like-minded societies in most East Coast cities, all funded by the Royal House of Saud."

"But enough of that," I say. "Did I mention Carol is a writer? She has several published spy novels."

"Carol Goodwin! That's where I heard your name. I'm a fan. I think I've read all your books," gushes Trixie.

After an hour or so of pleasant conversation, I mention that Carol and I have dinner reservations at the 'Carriage House Restaurant.' "Would you and Trixie like to join us," I ask Bill.

"Normally, I'd say yes. The Carriage House is a favorite of ours, but we will be tied up later this evening. Hopefully, another time."

As we drive away, "Perhaps they're into bondage," Carol says with a laugh. "That was a pleasant evening," she continues. "I'd like to see them again. Mabey dinner this weekend?"

5 Salt 'n Pepper

For the past year, year and a half, I have been a part of the Salt 'n Pepper Detective Agency. The agency was founded by two retired Boston police detectives; 'Salt,' Danny O'Kaye, a wiry Irishman, and Jimmy Anderson, the 'Pepper,' a former halfback from a small college in Alabama. He's big, he's black, and when provoked, mean. Maxie and I were invited to join the agency when my investigation into Fenk's attack intersected with their 'Missing Chinaman' case. The two cases morphed into the fentanyl threat against NYC's water supply.

As Carol and I wandered the Maine coast, Danny and Jimmy entertained a prospective new client. Two button-downed gents from Boston's British Consulate.

"Thank you for taking the time to meet with us." says the first. "I'm Basil Montgomery, and my companion is Clifford Steele. We are with the British Consulate General. We are looking for a private investigator to handle a rather delicate undertaking."

"Thanks for considering us," Danny responded. "Why us and not a more official inquiry to one of our government agencies?"

"As I said, it's delicate. We would like to avoid a fiasco like that caused by Clifford's brother Christopher. If you are interested, I'll provide the generalities, and then you can decide."

"Go ahead."

"As I said, we are with the British Government," continued Basil. "I assume you have heard of the Irish Republican Army and the unpleasantness it caused for many years. Well, we thought that problem had gone away. But no, it's been replaced by several

11

splinter groups, the most notable being 'The Provisionals.' The group du jour is the 'Irish Republican Liberation Army.' This group disavows the 1922 Easter Peace Agreement; they are looking to overturn it. Leaders in both the UK and the Irish Republic have branded them as terrorists. The IRLA's goal is to reunite all of Ireland as a single entity under its leadership."

We believe two of their agents are in America looking to buy arms. We want them. We want you to find them. Is this a case you can handle?"

"We can give it a try, but no guarantees," said Jimmy.

"Okay, but no press. Here are the folders with details on the two. Based on past experience and local sentiments, we believe they are in New England. And please keep your queries as discreet as possible."

After the two left, Danny says, "I guess we have a new client ... MI-6."

***

When I returned to our nondescript office above a Beacon Hill bookstore on Charles Street, I was greeted by a new face. Coming up the stairs, Maxie, well ahead of me, I hear a hesitant voice, "You must be Maxie. Sam, are you there?"

As I crest the top of the stairs, I see an attractive young lady sitting at the receptionist's desk, the desk I've been using for the past year. Danny kept threatening to hire a receptionist but never got around to it.

"You must be Sam," she said. "I'm Rosie. Jimmy said I was taking your desk, but they would work something out." Maxie was sniffing around the intruder, unsure what to make of her. "I hope Maxie and I will be friends," she said as she nervously eyed the dog.

"Danny's been threatening to hire a receptionist. It's nice to meet you. And as you've guessed, I'm Sam Goodmen, and this is Maxie."

"Maxi, 'bed,'" I commanded, and Maxie settled onto her dog bed in the corner. "Give her a day or so, and she will be eating out of your hand."

"I'm only here part-time," Rosie said. "I'm Jimmy's niece, Rosetta Tharpe."

"That name is vaguely familiar."

"Sister Rosetta Tharpe was a famous gospel singer in the '30s and 40s. My Uncle Jebali Tharpe claims a family relationship. My mother was a big fan, and now I'm saddled with the name," Rosie said.

About then, Danny steps out of the inner office. "Sam, I see you've met Rosie. She's Jimmy's niece and a student at Emerson College, majoring in theater. She'll be here between semester breaks and other times that she finds herself free."

"Now you need a place to sit. Jimmy found a small desk we could fit into the front office. It'll be snug, but the three of us are not often there at the same time. Or, we can convert our storage area into a small office, an option we offered when you first came on board."

"Or a third idea," I said, "Put the desk by Maxie's bed, and I can keep Rosie company. Besides, I'm not here all that much; some of us have to be out earning our keep."

"Funny, but talking about earning our keep, we have a new client. Come into the office, and I'll bring you up to date."

"The British Consulate General engaged us to locate some potential IRA terrorists. They believe two are in New England looking to buy arms for a new IRA splinter group, the Irish Republican Liberation Army," Danny starts.

"Jimmy is visiting a former IRA member, Danny O'Toole. He renounced the group in the late 90s and was on their hit list for several years. He's in his late eighties and living in Worcester with his grandson's family."

"Basil Montgomery, our contact, provided us with files on two of the terrorists," said Danny as he handed me their files. "Take a few minutes and look through these."

The first was for Seamus O'Neil, probably an alias. The attached photo showed a big bruiser with a buzz cut and a massive mustache. He's thought to be in his midthirties, a former boxer, and a possible IRA enforcer.

The second file was that of Michael Collins. "A likely alias," said Danny. "That name is most likely taken from the twentieth century Irish revolutionary leader." The picture stapled to the folder was that of an average-sized, lean-body man probably in his early 40s.

13

"Before becoming involved with the 'Provisionals,' MI-6 thinks he was an actor with Irish theaters in Dublin."

"A couple of charmers," I finally said. "What's our plan?"

6 A Lead

"While we wait for Jimmy to return," said Danny, "I'm visiting the 'Irish Social Club' but doubt I'll find much there. I have an old undercover contact working the bar. He might have heard some rumors. Why don't you take the morning and see what you can learn about the IRA ... background material?"

Great, I'm going back to school. I take a seat at Jimmy's desk, fire up the computer and plunge into the internet. What I found was a history of a people seeking independence from England that, in the twentieth century, descended into warring factions. The original Irish Republican Army, Sinn Féin, Provisional Irish Republican Army, and other variations; and the 'Troubles' spanning three decades."

The Troubles was a sectarian conflict between Ulster Protestants, the Orangemen, and Irish Catholics, the Republicans. It was not a religious conflict. The Protestants wanted Northern Ireland to remain within the United Kingdom. Irish nationalists wanted Northern Ireland to leave the United Kingdom and join a united Ireland. The Troubles span thirty years, '60s to the '90s, with some bleed over into the twenty-first century.

Rosie sticks her head in asking if we'd like some coffee. If not, she would be out for a few hours, a potential audition for a new stage show Emerson is sponsoring.

***

"Sam," Danny calls out as he enters the social club's bar. Sam Wilson is well into his seventies and still wiping the bar with his towel. "I haven't seen you for ages. I think the last time was when you were working at the Shamrock."

15

"Danny, you old bastard! It was you and your people who busted the Shamrock for gambling and sent the owners to Walpole and put me out of work."

"I got a promotion out of it," Danny said, "but I'm not here to rehash old stories. What can you tell me about the IRA?"

"Not much. Since the end of the Troubles, The Provisionals have been quiet. Several splinter groups, mostly in Ireland, have been making minor headlines, but you can find those yourself."

"Anything about an Irish Republican Liberation Army?"

"No," says Sam. "I've pretty much lost touch with the extremists." Bending over the bar and in a low voice says, "You want to ask Conor McGrath. You can find him at O'Neil's Bar down by the docks. And don't mention my name."

***

Late in the day, Jimmy returns to find Sam at his desk. "Where's Rosie?" were his first words as he walked in. "The girl's supposed to be at the desk out front."

"She's your niece? How can someone so cute be related to an ugly SOB like you? She said something about an audition."

"And Danny?"

"At the Irish Social Club. And before you ask, I'm doing a little research on the IRA and its variants."

There are footsteps on the stairs. Maxie is waging her tail as Danny gets to the top. Coming into the office, his first question is, "Did you find anything of interest in Worcester?"

"Nothing of real interest other than a name, an old-timer named Conor McGrath. O'Toole didn't know where we could find him or even if he was still alive,"

"I just came from the Irish Social Club," said Danny. My contact there also pointed us to Conor McGrath. He's still alive and can be found at O'Neil's Bar."

Looking at me, Danny asks, "Any new insights?"

"The Irish have the makings of a dysfunctional family that would make an interesting holiday gathering."

"Let's lock up; happy hour is calling," said Jimmy, "let's give O'Neil's a try."

"I'll leave you two to it," I said. "Carol has a special evening planned. And get that smirk off your face. She wants me at her latest book release. It is being sponsored by the 'Boston Literary District.' If I skip it, I'll be sleeping on the cot in the storage room."

7 Conor McGrath

O'Neil's Bar, located not far from the dock area, was what one expects of an Irish bar. Paraphernalia from the old country on the walls. Flags and sports trophies. And pictures of notable Irish freedom fighters, playwrights, and authors.

The evening crowd was dribbling in. The kitchen was gearing up with food items that would be asked for later that evening. Danny and Jimmy took a booth in the back of the room. Jimmy attracted a few glances as they came in, but he was soon forgotten.

As they sat, the waitress was at their side, "What can I get you?

"Something from the tap," says Jimmy, "half 'n half."

She looks at him with a puzzled look.

"Half stout and half bitters," explains Jimmy.

"Now you've done it," says Danny as the waitress walked away to place their order. "That's an English concoction popular in Liverpool."

She returns with two pints, somewhat less friendly. Danny tries to rekindle her initial welcoming smile with small talk and finally asks if the kitchen was open.

"Just opened," she said.

"And what would you recommend?"

"The Reuben sandwich is always good."

"We'll take two," Danny said.

"I don't care for corned beef," Jimmy mutters after the waitress leaves.

Ten minutes later, she delivers their order; Jimmy looks at it and thanks her. "Looks good," he says, and holding up his mug asks if they could get an Irish ale this time.

When she returns with the two ales, Danny asks, "Is Mr. McGrath in? I understand he's the owner."

If Jimmy's earlier request for half 'n half garnered a frosty reception, Danny's question got a glacier-like stare and the waitress's quick departure.

"Well, now you've done it," Jimmy says as they see the barman lay down his towel and head toward their booth.

"Understand you're asking about Conor. What's your interest?"

Danny, not one to beat about the bush, introduces the two of them. "We're PIs. Our client got wind of IRA aspirants' interest in buying weapons. He thought that was all a thing of the past. A couple of our inquiries suggest Conor might have some information that would either confirm or deny the rumor."

"We can't help you. Just finish your beer and move along," he says in less than a friendly voice.

"Okay, we can do that," says Danny. Turning to Jimmy, "I guess that leaves us with Captain Callahan in the morning; she heads up the Boston Police Department's terrorist task force." Looking back to the barkeep, "We really did prefer to keep this simple." Finishing his ale in two gulps, starts to get up …

Hold on, the bartender motions with his hands. "Conor is in the back office; let me talk to him."

Five minutes later, an old man with a cane emerges from the door behind the bar. The bartender points to Danny and Jimmy. He hobbles over to the booth and sits on the chair the bartender placed at the end of the booth.

"Salt 'n Pepper, PIs now?" he starts with a chuckle. "What was it ten, twelve years ago you tried to shut me down for gambling?"

Danny slowly realizes Conor McGrath is no stranger. He recalls the city's big push to eliminate backroom gambling a decade ago. Gaining some notoriety, Salt 'n Pepper had busted several establishments in Chinatown, Little Italy, and a few Irish pubs. "Yes, it's coming back to me now," said Danny.

19

"No hard feelings here," said Conor. The gambling was getting to be troublesome. IRA supporters kept pushing for a percentage. They weren't pleasant people. The judge gave me a hefty fine and probation. It all worked out."

"Now tell me, why are you looking for the IRA now?"

Danny repeats his story, this time showing pictures of Seamus O'Neil and Michael Collins. Conor called the bartender over to take a look; neither recognized the two.

After talking a bit longer with Conor, they left O'Neil's with one new lead. Conor had observed, "If these two plan to move weapons, they needed transportation. Back in the day, some of us used fishing trawlers out of Gloucester to move contraband to Ireland. My contact was Captain 'Red' O'Malley, but that was over a quarter century ago, and he was an old man then."

8 Misleading Lead

"How was the book release last night?" asks Danny. "You missed a good Reuben sandwich. Jimmy even got a bite or two down for the team."

Jimmy grunts, "A disgusting sandwich, a waste of good sauerkraut."

"Conor McGrath is well past his prime. Turns out Jimmy and I arrested him many years ago. Fortunately, he's not holding a grudge," Danny says as he goes on. "He did ask one interesting question; how do they plan to move the weapons? Air freight? UPS? …"

"Conor gave us the name of the fishing trawler captain he used to move contraband to Ireland in the '80s and '90s. His contact, if still alive, would be well over a hundred years old. But Conor's question was good. How do Seamus and Michael plan to move weapons to Ireland? Mabey, the trawler captain had a partner or a family member who picked up the trade. I'm thinking we need to take a trip up to Gloucester," said Danny.

There's a knock on the door, and Rosie comes in with a peace offering for her early departure yesterday; coffee and Danish.

"I left early yesterday for an audition. Emerson is sponsoring a play by a new Irish playwright," Rosie said. "I got the part! But I'll have to be there for rehearsals every afternoon. I'll have to give up this job."

Danny and Jimmy exchange glances, "We'll put you on half-time, just the mornings," Jimmy says.

Rosie is overjoyed and walks around the room, giving each of us a hug. As she passes me, she sees Michael Collins's folder open and his picture front and center. She stops and stares.

"Uncle Jimmy, that's the play's technical adviser," she says, pointing to Michael's picture.

Danny perks up at this, "Are you sure?"

Rosie picks up the picture and, after studying it, "Yes, he was introduced to us as a critic from Dublin who would be advising us on this production. But his name is Hugh Riddell."

Jimmy looking at Rosie, says, "Don't mention this to anyone! This is important. We can't tell you more, but please keep it to yourself."

As Rosie leaves the room, I mutter, "That's interesting."

"We need a work plan for the rest of the week," Danny says. "I'll call Basil and tell him we may have found one of his terrorists and invite him to join us when we confront him. I suggest one of us take this task on while the other two visit Gloucester."

"I'll work with Basil," says Jimmy.

"Okay, Sam, you up for a trip in the morning? In the meantime, I'll do a little online research and see what I can find on Captain 'Red' O'Malley."

***

Jimmy and Basil Montgomery meet at 'The Cutler Majestic Theatre' on Tremont Street the following afternoon. The new production, 'The Ripe Turnip,' is having its first rehearsal in the back of the theatre.

"The Ripe Turnip, what kind of play is that?" asks Basil.

"Rosie tells me it's about an Irish immigrant in New York and is a play on the phrase 'just fell off the turnip truck,'" says Jimmy.

"I may have to skip this one, but if our boy is here, I may reconsider," said Basil.

The two make their way to the back, find the director, and ask about the Irish critic.

"You mean Hugh Riddell? Let me get him for you."

"RIDDELL" he yells.

22

"Yo," and our person of interest emerges from behind a rack of costumes.

"Two men to see you, one from the British Consulate."

Jimmy introduces himself to Riddell and asks if he has ever heard of Michael Collins, showing him Seamus's picture. "You're a spitting image," Jimmy says.

"What's Gavin done now? We're identical twins. I often catch his crap. The last I heard he was in Belfast. Your friend here, from the British Consulate, if I heard right, suggests Gavin 's involved with the IRA ... again."

9 Gloucester

Danny and I are on the road by nine. I've left Maxie home; Danny didn't want dog hairs in his classic '87 Mustang.

The car was cherry red. Danny bought it with his signing bonus. In the late '80s police departments were having trouble recruiting and retaining officers due to the racial riots. Danny was just coming off his first contract; he signed on for another six years. He kept the car in a rented garage and treated it better than most parents treat their kids.

We arrived at Gloucester's commercial dock area late in the morning. Before leaving, I searched the internet for information on 'Red' O'Malley. I found his obituary, which I summarized for Danny:

"Red died a decade ago. His given name was William S. O'Malley. The obit did not say what the 'S' was for. He died of natural causes. Red was a mainstay of the Gloucester fishing fleet. He captained several trawlers over his years at sea, most of which were berthed in Harbor Cove. The last and his favorite was the Shamrock, a 58-foot diesel-powered craft carrying a crew of four. Red was survived by two sons, William Jr. and Robert."

Using my phone's GPS, we found Harbor Cove. The Harbor Master's 'shack' was located on the backside of the parking lot, overlooking the docks. Entering, we found a young man hunched over the desk reading the daily paper, coffee mug in hand. As we entered, a bell above the door tinkled, and he turned to us, making it obvious his previous position was caused by a deformity.

24

"Good morning, gentlemen. What can I do for you today? I'd get up, but it's difficult on some days."

"Good morning," Danny replied, and seeing a name plaque on the desk, added, "Mr. Huxley. Aren't you kind of young to be the Harbor Master?"

"I get that a lot. My father was the old Harbor Master ... for over twenty years. He retired, and a suitable replacement couldn't be found. I spent many years here with my father, knew the operation and most of the people on the docks. Three years ago, I convinced the dock owners to let me have a go at the job. It's worked out. Now what can I do for you?"

Danny introduced us, telling Mr. Huxley we were PIs glossing over any mention of the IRA, gun running, and British intelligence; merely saying we were looking for information. "Do you know or remember Captain Red O'Malley? I think he captained the Shamrock."

"Red. Yes, he was a real character. He told all kinds of wild tales to us kids. He died, let me think, over a decade ago. His eldest son, ltl Red, now captains the Shamrock."

"Where can we find ltl Red?" Danny asks.

"The Shamrock is a large trawler; we put it over on Dock 5, on the harbor side. It's a hike from here. You might want to drive. There's parking at the end of the jetty."

We thanked him and drove to Dock 5. On the harbor side of the pier was an old trawler. Rust was winning the battle with the paint. The name Shamrock, painted on its stern, could just be made out. It was in need of some TLC.

As we approached the boat, four crew members idling on the dock challenged us, hostility in the air, "Who are you, and why are you here?"

"We're looking for O'Malley," Danny responds, and with that, the biggest of the four throws down his cigarette and takes a few steps toward us.

Danny introduced us, he was Alex Johnson, and I was Walter Allen. We were with a group in Boston who wished to move some goods down the coast. We were told ltl Red could help.

"And who told you that," said whom we assumed was ltl Red.

As Danny was hesitant in answering, one of the other idlers yelled, "They're probably Feds!"

That set ltl Red off, sucker-punching Danny. The other two attacked me. When I woke, I found we had been dragged back to the parking lot. I was sore but mostly intact. Danny, on the other hand, was hurting. He mumbled something about his car keys. I found them in his pocket, loaded him into the car, and we made an ignoble retreat.

Stopping on the roadside, I suggested we get him to a hospital. "No," Danny insisted on returning to Boston. By the time we got to the suburbs, he was delirious. Without asking, I took him to Boston Central's emergency receiving area. Upon seeing Danny, the medical techs loaded him onto a gurney and rushed him into the ER.

Danny had a mild concussion, three broken ribs, and possibly other internal injuries. I called Jimmy and told him where we were, details to be provided when he got to the hospital. While waiting for Jimmy, Lieutenant Doyle, a friend, and a Boston police detective happened by; he was checking on the status of a perp he had dropped off earlier who had a few gunshot wounds.

Doyle and Danny go way back. "What happened?"

"A dockside brawl in Gloucester. We were talking with a trawler's crew; they became agitated." About then, Jimmy arrived. I went over the morning's events for both of them. Jimmy then provided Doyle with some background on the case we were working.

Doyle was a little pissed that the British Consulate had bypassed city authorities. Still, there was nothing to be done about that. "Gloucester is outside my jurisdiction. I have a few friends up there that owe me favors," Doyle said. "Let me know how I can help."

***

By unspoken mutual agreement Jimmy and I met up in the morning. "All set?" he asks.

"Yes," I say as we got into my SUV. We were out of the city twenty minutes later, heading north to Gloucester.

I parked at the end of Dock 5. Getting out of the vehicle, I saw the same four guys by the Shamrock positioning some boxes in a sling to be loaded aboard the boat.

"Hay shitheads," I yelled out; we've got some business to finish.

26

They turn, look at me, and ltl Red yells, "You back for another beating?"

Jimmy steps out on the other side of the SUV, walks around, and joins me.

"Look, he's brought his big n…r with him. I'm scared now," one of the others says laughingly.

As Jimmy and I take a few steps forward, ltl Red, the crew rapidly advancing. I have my hand on the key fob in my pocket and press the rear hatch release. As it starts to lift up, there is a flash of black and tan, driving two white incisors down the dock. One of Red's crew jumps off the pier to escape Maxie. The second throws his arm up just in time to take the brunt of Maxie's weight and is on his back, Maxie with a firm grip on his forearm. The third retreats down the pier to retrieve a makeshift weapon. Red takes on Jimmy, who delivers a solid haymaker, resulting in pennies exploding from Jimmy's fist. Red is out cold. The third man is running at Maxie, a metal bar in his hand, ready to deliver a damaging blow. I intercept him, giving a solid punch to his kidneys, followed by a knee to the face when he doubles over.

Jimmy turns to me, "This took less than sixty seconds. What was your problem yesterday," he says, grinning. Pull these guys behind those boxes so we can question them without an audience. Did you bring the zip ties?"

As we're laying the three out in a somewhat secluded spot the fourth crew member is climbing back onto the dock. Maxie and I retrieved him, adding him to our collection.

As ltl Red revives, I start, "Yesterday, we were asking about moving some 'hot' merchandise down the coast. As my partner said, we had a good source saying you did this type of thing. And then you went all bullshit! We'd like some answers today."

"Who are you hauling goods for?" I ask. "What kind of goods?" I just get a defiant glare from ltl Red.

Looking at the four, I figured the one having the first encounter with Maxie might be the loose link. I brought Maxie over to him and gave the command "Interrogate." Maxie straddles him, snout inches from his face growling. "Okay, if you want to keep your face, who was your customer?"

27

"Shut the f...k up," sputters Red through his broken jaw.

Jimmy kicks Red in the ribs, and I could swear I heard bones snap.

Turning back, I give Maxie another command, "Nip."

Maxie takes a little nip on his cheek, not quite breaking the skin.

Our interrogatee is now in a panic and can't talk fast enough.

"A guy nicknamed 'The Greek' in Atlantic City. We're hauling whiskey for him. We pick it up in Canada and deliver it to New Jersey."

"Where is the whiskey now?" I ask, nudging Maxie, who growls.

"On the boat, fifty cases of Canadian Club," he yelps.

Over the next few minutes, he tells us of two Irishmen looking to hire the Shamrock. They wanted to know if she could make it to Ireland, how much cargo could she hold, etc.

Jimmy looks at me, giving me a thumbs up, and asks me to keep our guest quiet. He then calls Basil and tells him what we have. "Can you get some federal officers here to take our new friends into custody? I don't think you want the local police involved. The resulting press coverage would not be helpful."

An hour later an FBI helicopter set down in the parking area. Two agents emerged and started down the dock to us. One is an imposing-looking female. Looking at me, she says, "Sam, we meet again and that must be Maxie. Lieutenant Doyle told me about you and your innovative integration techniques. Clearly, exaggeration on his part," she said with a smile.

"I'm Agent Joyce Bixby. Basil Montgomery, our MI-6 contact, alerted us to a possible smuggling operation. He said you were detaining some people of interest that we might like to talk with. What can you two add?"

Jimmy leads her over to where we had the 'people of interest' while telling her our story.

"That's kind of weak for us to hold them," Joyce says. "What else do you have?"

"How about the fifty cases of liquors on the trawler?"

Joyce sends one of the agents to look in the boat's hold.

He yells down to Joyce, "The hold is full of Canadian Club; damn, I need to find out where they're fishing."

28

"And," I continue, "here is a recorded confession." I press playback on my iPhone.

10 Walpole

A week later Danny is back in the office, looking like crap, but back in the office. "Okay, where are we? We've bagged one trawler full of whiskey," and muttering under his breath, "weren't quick enough to score a case of Canadian Club for ourselves."

Looking at Jimmy, "Your niece sent us down a rabbit hole with Michael Collin's twin, Hugh Riddell. But at least we got Michael's real name, Gavin Riddell."

Jimmy adds, "Conor McGrath asked a good question, how do they plan to move the weapons to Ireland? I'd add a second question to that, where are they planning on getting the weapons?"

About then Doyle comes up the stairs, not having met Rosie before he flashes his badge and announces he's a city tax collector. "Miss. if you would, please tell Mr. O'Kaye his company owes the city $3,221, payable now."

Rosie calls the inner office, "Danny, there is a creep out here saying you owe the city money."

The inner door bursts open with Jimmy fuming, seeing Doyle he breaks out laughing. "Rosie, this is Lieutenant Doyle. Next time he's here, call the health department," he says as he comes over to shake Doyle's hand. "Come back to the inner sanctum. Danny is there; we can update you on the case."

Taking a seat, Doyle starts by telling us, "Joyce is ecstatic about busting the booze smuggling ring. Yesterday the Treasury Department busted 'The Greek' for tax evasion. And yes, she gave Maxie full credit."

30

"But that's not why I'm here. I want to see how you're doing Danny. That was a nasty beating they gave you."

"I'm doing good.

"Are you up for a little field trip tomorrow," Doyle asks Danny. "I'm making my monthly trip to Walpole. Perhaps Flanagan, the guy I'm visiting, might shed some light on the Irish mob."

"How so?" says Danny.

"Henry Flanagan was a member of the old Irish mob. Its members are mostly in the ground now. He's serving a life sentence for murder; took out some of his competition with a car bomb in the '80s. I grew up with his son, Gerald known to us as 'Jerry.' When his father was convicted, my mother looked after him. In college, we both were in ROTC, and commissioned in the Massachusetts National Guard. We both stayed in as reservists and were called up just in time for Operation Iraqi Freedom.

"Jerry was my best friend; we had each other's back. In 2004 we deployed to Bagdad. Our first mission was to clear a neighborhood of the bad guys. He led his platoon down one street, and I took my platoon down the adjacent street. We were making good progress until the blast. I saw a large column of smoke; my radioman received an urgent call from his counterpart. 'Immediate backup was needed. Half his men were down.' I dispatched three squads down one of the adjoining alleyways. The final count was seven dead and twelve wounded. Jerry was one of the dead.

"When I returned home, I visited Henry in Walpole. He knew his son was dead but not the details. I spent over an hour with him recounting my time with Jerry as teenagers, in college, and later in the guard. We bonded in some way ... and I've been visiting him monthly since then. So, are you up for a trip tomorrow?"

Walpole is a maximum-security prison, one of the most violent in the Nation. It has hosted several notable inmates, one being the Boston Strangler. It was opened in '55, and with riots in the '90s and later gross mismanagement, it is now scheduled for closure with inmates to be sent to other more 'humane' institutions.

That Wednesday, when we arrived, the prison population was down by about two-thirds from its peak. Prisoners remaining were

31

mostly nonviolent, held there at the courts' direction, or elderly. Henry Flanagan fell into the last category, being an octogenarian.

Without much delay, we were ushered into the visiting area. Doyle requested we be allowed to use one of the integration rooms for privacy since our visit would touch on a current police matter. Being a frequent visitor, well known to the staff, the request was quickly granted.

After sitting ten minutes in a nondescript room, Henry was finally brought in. He was a small elderly man radiating confidence.

After introducing me and outlining my current case, Doyle asks, "Henry what are their plans for you next year?"

"Well, if I'm still alive," he answers with a chuckle, "rumor has it that me and a few of the other old-timers may have our sentences commuted and be sent to a halfway house."

"That would be nice," said Doyle. "I don't think you'll be a threat to the public, and the Governor will get compassion points from the left."

Henry, turning to me, "You've probably been told I have ties to the old Irish mob. Well, that's true, and they are mostly dead. Back in my day, we did some business with the IRA. It was always iffy. They were a bloodthirsty group. If they thought you crossed them, you weren't seen again."

Doyle probably brought you along today hoping I'd give you a lead or two. That's taking me back thirty or more years. Those leads are dead, or the few remaining are in prison. The only tidbit that might be useful is an IRA safe house in Quincy. Patrick Nee, an Irish Republican sympathizer, had a place out on Houghs Neck. Last I heard he was in prison, but the house? It might be worth looking into."

"One other thing. Back in the day, there was a reporter that championed the IRA. I cut out his articles. The guy had no clue, but he made us look good. If he is still around, he could provide you with a few leads."

"Do you have a name?" Danny asked.

"No. He was with a New York paper, New York Times I think."

Later, back in the office, Danny turns to Jimmy, "Where did Sam go?"

32

"Took Maxie to the vet, annual checkup."

"Okay, when he gets back I need him to track down some property records in Quincy." You and I need to see what we can find out about Patrick Nee and talk with his compatriots if they are still with us. Lieutenant Doyle will provide us with Nee's police record."

Jimmy looks at Danny, "Yas-sir boss man, we all hopping to your commands."

"Sorry for the abruptness; just got carried with these new leads," says a chastised Danny. "What are your thoughts?"

"Nothing, you've got it covered, but a conversation is nice."

11 A New Direction

"While you guys were out, the FBI called," says Rosie. "An agent named Joyce Bixby wants one of you to call her back."

Looking at me, Danny says she's Maxie's friend. Sam, maybe you should call her.

I punched some numbers on my cell, "This is Sam Goodwin. I'm with the Salt 'n Pepper Detective agency and am returning Agent Bixby's call from yesterday."

I'm put on hold. A moment later Agent Bixby is on the line. "Mr. Goodwin, I was following up on ltl Red's arrest last month. I'd like to invite you and Mr. Anderson, and Mr. Doyle, if he's up for it, down to be interviewed about the events in Gloucester. Would tomorrow be convenient, tomorrow morning?" she asks.

Rosie's looking at us, "What did you guys do?"

The FBI's field office is in Chelsea, on the north side of Boston. Street and the railroad tracks. Fighting the inbound commuter traffic, we arrive at the office in time to find a local Dunkin' Donuts to get fortified for the upcoming integration. Parking is not a problem; the Feds can afford large parking lots.

At the security desk, we are asked about our business there.

"Agent Bixby invited us down for a talk," Jimmy replies.

The guard places a call and after a few muffled words on the phone, turns to us, "Have a seat over there," pointing to a seating area. "Agent Bixby will be right down."

I'm just finishing my coffee as Bixby emerges from the elevator and comes through the turnstile.

"Thank you for coming down," she said as if we had a choice. "I have a few questions that I think you can help me with. Let's go to the conference room upstairs."

"Well, at least it's not an integration room," I whisper to Danny.

We are ushered into a small conference room. The table could probably manage ten or so people. There are two men, about my age already there. Agent Bixby makes introductions. "The man on your right, Agent Jones, is the Agent in Charge of the Boston field office, my boss. Across from him is Agent Wilson from the Bureau of Alcohol, Firearms, and Tobacco."

We are seated, coffee offered, and pleasantries exchanged. Agent Jones is the first to get to the topic at hand. "Can you tell us what brought you to Gloucester and ltl Red?"

So, Danny starts at the beginning. The mention of MI-6 raises some eyebrows, but no comments. After ten or fifteen minutes, Danny covers most of the high points. As for the IRA agents, all Danny can tell is our discovery that Michael Collins's real name is Gavin Riddell and that he is Hugh Riddell's twin, which leads to a discussion about The Ripe Turnip. We provided Bixby with the photos Basil gave us. A picture of 'Hugh' from the theater production as well as my description of Gavin with a beard.

As for the second agent, Seamus O'Neil, we can add nothing, only the photo Basil gave us and my description of 'Mr. Clean.'

There are some questions by Wilson and Jones to tease out bits of data, but that line of discussion soon leads to a dead end.

"We are indebted to you for finding that bootleg booze. It was coming from Canada and going to casinos in New Jersey ... skipping import duties," said Agent Wilson.

"Ltl Red's crew flipped after we removed ltl Red from the scene. We offered them a deal, put agents on the trawler, and had the crew make the scheduled delivery to The Greek. We've been after that bastard for years."

"It looks like you guys are facing two major questions," said Agent Jones. "The first, how to move the weapons? Your lead to ltl Red was spot on. But that is no longer viable given we've impounded the Shamrock. They'll need another ship if that is, in fact, their choice of transportation.

"The second question is, 'where are they getting the weapons from?' We might have a lead for you. We and the ATF have been tracking stolen military weapons from Fort Drum. I'll ask our field office in upstate New York to provide assistance if you think that lead is worth exploring. Personally, I think it is."

12 Fort Drum

Back on Charles Street, we are mulling over the leads we now have.

"Henry Flanagan pointed us to Patrick Nee," said Danny. There might be something there, or not.

"The FBI raised another interesting question, where are the weapons coming from?" continued Danny. "They pointed us to Ft. Drum and were kind enough to provide an FBI contact in Watertown that might be able to help us.

"If there is no objection, Jimmy and I will go to Fort Drum and see what we can dig up. Sam, can you follow up on Patrick Nee?"

Danny calls Rosie into the office, "I've got an assignment for you. You will probably have to spend the next few days at the library; I doubt the New York Times's online database goes back to the nineties. What I'm looking for are articles on the IRA from the later part of that decade. Just print them out. No need to take notes on them."

***

Fort Drum is in upstate New York and is the home of the 10th Light Infantry Division and various Army National Guard battalions. A lot of weapons are available. The question is, are they being pilfered?

The Bureau maintains a small satellite office in Watertown on the sixth floor of the Dulles State Office Building. There are no access restrictions to the building other than a sleeping guard in the lobby. Danny scans the list of building tenants posted by the elevator, Jimmy pushes the elevator call button, and moments later the two walk into the FBI office.

The receptionist, looking like a high school student sporting pink hair and wearing a flower shirt, asks what they need. "We would like to speak with Agent Hammond if he's in," Danny tells the young man.

On the office intercom, he announces, "Nick, you have some visitors at the front desk."

This level of professionalism causes Jimmy to roll his eyes just as a middle-aged man approaches to lead them into the back office spaces.

"Hired help is hard to come by here. We don't want to make it more difficult by requiring competency. I'm Agent Nathaniel Hammond. The Boston Field Office said you may be stopping in. And as you heard, I go by Nick."

Coffee is offered and declined as Nick asks what he can do for them.

Danny briefly summarizes their case, finishing with, "Agent Jones told us about stolen weapons at Fort Drum, suggesting our Irish radicals may be here looking to buy some weapons."

"It's possible but not likely," Nick says. We've shut that spigot off. The two enlisted men caught stealing the weapons are in the stockade. Their customers were a group of Canadians wanting to arm the Canadian Revolutionary Brigade."

Both Danny and Jimmy look puzzled.

Nick goes on, "The Canadian Revolutionary Brigade is an extreme right group that is opposing, to use their words, Trudeau's authoritarian government. It's a relatively new group, formed after Trudeau's crackdown on truckers last year."

Jimmy said to Danny, "This may have been a long trip for nothing. But if weapons were stolen once, why not again. I think we should look around to find other sources. Nick, where would you look?"

"Mildred's Biker Bar. It's up on Rt 11, a mile this side of the main gate. The Dead Head Cycle Club hangs out there along with bike enthusiasts from the base. Not the friendliest place to visit."

That evening Danny and Jimmy pull into Mildred's parking lot. There are a dozen or so bikes parked by the entrance. Inside there is

38

the expected bar and pool table and several empty tables. Most of the patrons are at the bar betting on the pool game.

The two PIs grab stools at the end of the bar and order beer. Watching the game, Jimmy says in a not-so-quiet voice, "They play like pansies."

Two big bruisers sitting nearby start to take offense getting off their stools. One of the players telling them to hold off turns to Jimmy, "Think you can do better? Tell you what I'll do. If you can beat me, two out of three games, the two of you can walk out of here in one piece."

Now the bar patrons are placing bets; odds are greatly against Jimmy. Danny takes out a hundred dollars and bets on Jimmy at ten-to-one. Danny was betting Jimmy's skills had not diminished since retiring. Jimmy, a known pool hustler in various Boston Police Department precincts, was selecting his cue.

The balls were racked, and the two players lag to see who breaks. Jimmy wins the break and then proceeds to clear the table. In the second game, the house player makes a valiant effort but fails in the end.

Danny goes to collect his winning, and that's when things get ugly.

The house player takes a swing at Jimmy with his pool cue. Jimmy steps aside and breaks his cue over his head. As mentioned earlier, Jimmy is not small, and Danny works out in the local boxing gym when time permits. The bar erupts into chaos. Danny and Jimmy, standing back-to-back level all-comers.

Mildred's Biker Bar is known for its frequent brawls, and the Watertown police quickly arrive. Everyone is arrested, including Danny and Jimmy.

Danny's one call is to Nick. Two hours later Agent Hammond is able to convince the desk Sargent that Danny and Jimmy are undercover, working for the FBI.

Those two hours waiting for Nick gave Danny the opportunity to ask his fellow jailbirds where he could buy military-grade weapons.

One of his more talkative cellmates identified Sargent Nonnamaker as the man to see. He's an armorer with the National Guard.

As the three left the Watertown lockup, Danny proudly announced the night was not in vain; he had the name of a potential weapons supplier, a Sargent Nonnamaker.

Nick starts to laugh, "Nonnamaker is one of the two enlisted men I mentioned earlier. He's in the stockade."

Somewhat discouraged, Danny asks Agent Hammond if it could be arranged for him and Jimmy to speak with Nonnamaker.

"Come by the office in the morning and I'll see what can be arranged."

After a quick stop at the Waffle House, the two PIs are back at the Dulles State Office Building where they find Nick on the phone. As he hangs up, he tells them, "That was the Post Provost Marshal. Our kids are in the same junior high classes. I was calling in a favor, getting you two into the stockade to interview Nonnamaker. He agreed, if you'd sit down with him afterward for a debriefing.

"Gladly, when can we do this?" asks Jimmy.

"After lunch. He'll have passes waiting for you at the main gate."

Fort Drum is much like other Army bases. The MPs at the gate have the promised passes and provide directions to the stockade.

The stockade is on the far side of the base, inside its own fenced area. The guard there is expecting them, directing them to a parking space by the main entrance. Going into the reception area, they are met by Colonel Stewart, the Post Provost.

"Good afternoon gentlemen. This is somewhat unusual, but you've perked my curiosity. As agreed, you'll provide me with details, yes? Sargent Bowman here will take you back to our interview room. I look forward to our discussion."

Bowman leads the two down a short hall to a small room with a table and three chairs. Nonnamaker is already there, hands handcuffed to the table.

"Sargent Nonnamaker, thank you for meeting with us," says Danny.

"It will be Private Nonnamaker soon," the man says. "My court-martial is in two weeks; I'll be busted to E-1, then off to the Army prison at Fort Leavenworth. I understand you want to talk about theft of military weapons. The stupidest thing I ever did."

We spent a half hour talking with him about how he was contacted. How the weapons were stolen. And how he planned to deliver them. We asked if there were other customers, perhaps with Irish accents.

"No, just the Canucks," Nonnamaker said. "They made it sound so easy, and the money ... the stupidest thing I ever did," he repeats.

As they left the interview room, Danny said, "Well, that was about useless. That schmuck has f...k his life up for the promise of a few dollars."

Sargent Bowman escorted them to a conference room where the Colonel was waiting. He has coffee available, his mug full and in front of him, two empty mugs sitting on the table and says as he pushes the mugs across the table, "Not the best coffee but it's hot," he says.

"I hope your visit was worth your time. The best I can make of it is he's a kid that made a dumb decision."

"I agree," Danny said. "He had no information that is of any use to us."

"Tell me," Colonel Stewart said, "what are you looking for?"

Danny goes through the full story with the Provost, telling him of the IRA's interest in acquiring weapons.

"They won't get them here," said the Colonel. "General Wells, the base commander, was incensed when he heard of the recent breach in security. He read the riot act to the base armorers. He's directed all future actions involving weapons to require two-man supervision. He's put the fear of god into them, almost to the point that when they take a crap, they go in pairs."

41

13 Houghs Neck

When Sam returned with Maxie's clean bill of health, Danny, on his way out the door with Jimmy on their way to Fort Drum, asked Sam to follow up on the Houghs Neck lead. Did Patrick Nee own property there, and if so, which lot?

Houghs Neck is an upscale neighborhood on a peninsula of the same name jutting into Boston Harbor. Quincy is its own city in the Boston metropolitan area, just south of Boston proper.

Sam headed home to drop Maxie off. His home is in Dorchester and is halfway to Quincy. Carol takes a break from her novel and the two have a quick lunch together. "Carol your next novel should have your Greek sleuth chasing Irish mobsters. I'll consult. This case has more tentacles than an octopus."

Sam is then off, headed for the Quincy town hall, specifically the land records office. According to the nameplate on her desk, the clerk is Mary Quigly. This gave Sam his opening. "Ms. Quigly, did your mother work for the Boston Police Department? The canine division?"

"Yes," came Mary's tentative reply.

"I'm Sam Goodwin, one of the dog handlers. Betsey retired a year before I did. How is she coping with retirement?"

"She is a committed grandmother." says Mary, who is now sporting a big grin, "looking after my two little ones. How can I help you?"

Sam explains he is now a PI and is looking for Mr. Patrick Nee's property records out on Houghs Neck.

"Patrick Nee, big in the Irish mob wasn't he?" Mary says. "He was big news around here a couple decades ago. The property wouldn't be in his name now; it would have been confiscated by the Feds. But let's look at old tax records to see what property he owned back then."

Mary goes into the back room and returns with a large ledger. Paging through it, she exclaims, "Here he is. He owned the property at 117 Edgewater Drive. Hold on a minute; let's see who owns it now." Mary turns to her computer keyboard and types in the address. "It's owned now by Henry Lee Woo. Definitely not Irish," she quips.

"Thanks, you've been a big help. Tell your mother hello for me and Maxie," I say as I collect my notes.

My next task is a 'drive-by' of 117 Edgewater Drive, where I find a large house separated from the bay by the Drive and a strip of parkland. It's a nice house, sitting by itself on the corner of Wall Street and Edgewater Drive. Cars are in the driveway, so I decided to stop.

Knocking on the door, there is no response. Knocking again, an elderly Chinese lady opens the door. She calls back into the house in Chinese; a middle-aged man comes to the door and steps out onto the porch with me. He looks familiar.

"Mr. Godwin," he starts, "what brings you here?"

I'm still at a loss. Sensing my confusion, he says, "I'm Henry Woo, owner of the Su Su Restaurant. If you recall, we had some unpleasant business last year regarding Middle Eastern men that frequented my restaurant."

"Yes," it's coming back to me now. "Thank you for your help; it helped to put away some ISIS terrorists. But that is not why I'm here. Your house was once owned by Patrick Nee, a famous Irish mobster. I'm trying to track down his past and his ties to the IRA. I don't suppose there was anything of his when you moved in?"

Henry stands there looking at me, somewhat indecisive. "I read about al-Qaradawi's murder and the fentanyl attack on New Your City's water supply. Were the men you were seeking at my restaurant part of this?"

"Yes."

Making his mind up, Henry says, "Come in. I want to show you something. We walk partway down the entry hall; he turns and presses the molding in the walnut woodwork. A panel beneath the stairs pops open. Inside is a small arsenal. Tommy guns, shotguns, pistols, etc. "My mother found this shortly after we moved in. She was polishing the woodwork ... almost had a heart attack. We don't know what to do with it."

"Let me call some people. You are not in trouble. As a matter of fact, you will probably get kudos for finding this stash."

I called Doyle. Quincy is not in his jurisdiction, but he can refer my call to the proper authorities, the FBI. A few minutes after I disconnected, he called back. Sit tight; the Feds are on their way.

It's midafternoon before the Feds arrive. Two black SUVs, nothing subtle. The first person out is Agent Joyce Bixby. I met her on the porch.

"Sam, you get around," were her first words.

"And good to see you again Agent Bixby."

"The Woo's bought this house many years ago. Henry Woo owns a restaurant in Chinatown, the Su Su. He helped in last year's takedown of the ISIS cell. At one time this house was owned by Patrick Nee. You remember the name, don't you?"

"Yes, an Irish mobster with ties to the IRA. It was my boss who arrested him two decades ago."

"And he tied up all the loose ends?" I ask as I lead Joyce into the hallway.

"So he claims," she says as I press the strip of molding, and the hidden door pops open. Her eyes pop when she sees the arsenal.

She calls her team leader over and directs him to take an inventory of the weapons.

Smiling, Joyce comments, "My boss is a pompous ass. He's not going to live this down. He should have caught this when he cleared the house."

To add to her amusement, I told her about a young rookie, three decades ago, being chastised for a similar oversight by his partner.

"I was new to the force and assigned to a senior foot patrolman. We busted some small-time hood. He told me to clear the house; I did and found nothing. He then led me to the staircase and told me to study it. I did and saw nothing. He asked, 'What's under the stairs?' He went on to explain many old houses had hidden spaces under the stairs. Carpenters during prohibition converted these spaces into booze cabinets, most with hidden latches ... like we have here. Tell your boss rookie BPD officers know this trick."

"Mr. Woo tells me his mother recently found the hiding place while polishing the woodwork. When the door sprung open, she almost had a heart attack. The family has been worried sick about what to do. They're from China. This kind of thing would put them in prison. Can you see that they get some positive accolades for the find?"

14 Abe's

The next day I'm reporting my findings to the team. "That arms stash could have been a good start for our Irish weapons smugglers, but there was no useful information on Patrick for us ... a dead end."

"As for Patrick Nee," I say, "he died ten years ago in Terre Haute, a federal prison. As for his buddies, they are all having a reunion in the great beyond. His girlfriend is in a senior living center over in Braintree. She has Alzheimer's; thinks Patrick was her father."

Well, you did better than us; we found nothing useful at Fort Drum. You at least got us some positive points with the Feds.

"Rosie will be in later this morning," reports Jimmy. "She found almost two dozen articles from the '90s having a positive slant on the IRA. She's going to screen the late '80s before calling it quits."

"Lieutenant Doyle gave me a copy of Nee's police record. I didn't see anything that could help us. The report is on my desk if you want to look at it."

"We're doing great," I observe. "Dead ends and dead people."

"On a positive note, Carol is having a book signing for her latest novel downstairs tomorrow. You are all invited. A small crowd could boost her coverage in the local papers."

It's midafternoon when Rosie returns. "Sorry for being late. I stopped for lunch, and some of my classmates wanted to know how the play was going. Speaking of which, we will be having a dress rehearsal on Friday, not this Friday, the following Friday. You are all invited."

She opens her backpack and pulls out a folder, a thick folder. "These are the articles I found with positive coverage of the IRA or splinter groups."

"And by the way, it's a pain to print copies from microfiche."

"The one thing that jumped out at me was the reporter. Most of these articles were written by Bill Hardy. He retired from the Times ten years ago."

"Bill Hardy," Rosie had my attention. "He's the journalist Carol and I met in Maine earlier this year."

***

Abe's Bookstore was on the first floor; we had the upper portion of the building and were Abe's tenants. Abe's wife, Cecile, managed the store. She is one of the prime movers of the Boston Literary District.

Carol's signing gig started at eleven and was scheduled for three hours. Danny and I were among the small group of her followers there to greet her.

Danny bought a signed copy of her book, 'The Artifact Smuggler.' The book's cover displayed a Greek-flagged freighter. "I thought the story was about a Greek intelligence agent battling the Turks. What does a freighter have to do with it?" asks Danny.

"A cover for smuggling, maybe. Read the book," says Carol.

As Danny and I are leaving, I call out, "Carol, come upstairs when you are done. We can go for a late lunch or an early dinner depending on how you are feeling,"

It's midafternoon when Carol mounts the top of the stairs and sees Rosie for the first time. "You must be Jimmy's niece; Sam's been telling me about you." Smiling, Carol adds, "He claims you are trying to steal my little girl's affection."

"Mrs. Goodwin. Maxie is in the front office with Sam. She's a real sweety, but I don't think I'm going to sway her loyalties. Go on in. They're expecting you."

As Carol enters the room, Danny relinquishes the one stuffed chair in the office, offering it to her. "You must be exhausted," he says. "Many sales?"

Maxie comes over and rubs up against her as she scratches the dog's ears. "Fifty books or so. Several of my old fans showed up. Where's Sam?"

"He stepped out to get some pastries and coffee to celebrate your book release," Jimmy said.

"I just met your niece, Jimmy. I hope you guys aren't corrupting her."

"She's part of the team," Sam says as he walks in.

As Carol looks around the office, the pictures of Michael Collins, a.k.a. Gavin Riddell, and Seamus O'Neil, posted on the bulletin board with the case's notes, catch her eye. She studies them, then asks for a magic marker and asks if it would be okay if she marked the pictures up.

"Have at it," Danny says as he hands her a marker.

She goes to Michael's picture and adds an unruly head of black hair and a neat beard. "Sam, who is this guy?"

He studies Carol's handiwork for a moment, "My god, that's one of the Irishmen we met in Maine two months ago."

"And the other one, if you remove the mustache and the buzzcut, it's 'Mr. Clean.'"

I stood there staring at the two photos muttering, "Right in front of me all this time."

15 Connections

"Bill Hardy, an IRA sympathizer, and Riddell and O'Neil all at Ocean Point at the same time. Not a coincidence," I'm saying to my partners the next morning. "For the past two months, we've been running in circles, following one false lead after another. I think we may have found a connection."

"Let's look into Hardy's background," says Jimmy. "We may find something of use. We should also ask Basil to give us whatever the British authorities have on Gavin Riddell now that we know that that is his real name. As for Seamus O'Neil, we may find him to be one of Gavin's buddies under a different name. I'll call Basil this morning."

"Okay, we got a plan," I say. "But I still have some misgivings about Hugh Riddell's story. If there is no objection, I'm going to dig into that. And Hardy, he's mine," I say.

As Danny and Jimmy start their respective taskings, I go to my desk in the outer office, "Rosie you're knowledgeable about social media platforms, aren't you?" I ask.

I want to see what's online about Hugh and Gavin Riddell. They are twins, born sometime in the late '80s or early '90s in either Northern Ireland or the Republic of Ireland.

"And which haystack do you want me to start in?" asks Rosie.

"Your choice. While you start your search, I'll start with one of the genealogy research sites."

Plucking away at my keyboard, I navigate to Ancestory.com's home page. "They want me to join," I say. "Seventy-five dollars for a one-month international membership gives me access to worldwide databases. Or three hundred fifty for the year."

I decide on the monthly membership, get registered, and sign in. I start with a wide search: Hugh Riddell, born in 1995 plus or minus five years, over fifteen pages in hits. I reduce the scope to the British Isles. Progress, only fourteen pages. I trim the search to Northern Island, and I'm rewarded with four pages. I try again with the Republic of Ireland and got three pages.

I next turn to Gavin Riddell, starting with Northern Island. Two pages. Searching the Republic of Ireland, I turn up three pages.

Short of brute force, looking at every hit, how do I correlate findings for the birth of the twins Hugh and Gavin? I bite the bullet and start with Northern Ireland. It's well into the late afternoon, and the monitor is becoming blurry. I'm skimming the Royal Victoria Hospital records when I see a March 21st, 1993 entry for the birth of twin boys to Margaret and John Riddell. This hit came up under Hugh's search. I flip to Gavin, the same time period, and there is the same entry. BINGO!

Digging deeper into genealogical records, I go back two generations for the parents. According to online Irish historical records, John's father, Gavin, and grandfather Lim were minor IRA members.

In 1969 Gavin played a role in establishing The Provisionals as the inheritors of the IRA banner. Gavin's team was ambushed by the Queen's Guard in '03. He was killed along with his son John, the father of Hugh and Gavin.

Lim died in a state nursing home, a broken and bitter old man, in 2014.

Margaret's maiden name was O'Shaughnessy. Her father, William O'Shaughnessy, a senior leader in The Provisionals, was captured by the Crown and is being held at HM Prison just outside Belfast. He had three daughters. Margaret, Ellen, and Grace, the youngest. Margaret was killed in a sectarian riot in 2004, leaving her two boys orphans.

Her grandfather, a minor player in the IRA, was killed in 1963 by 'Orange' militants in a street fight.

By the time I look up, I'm alone in the office. It's after seven. I give Carol a call, "I'll be late. Been doing some internet research. Found a lot of interesting information, not sure how it will help us find Gavin and his friend. Maxie and I will be home in an hour."

The next morning, I chided Rosie for abandoning me and gave her a quick recap of my findings. "Did you find anything?"

"I found an abandoned Facebook account. If it's Gavin's, he attended the University of Dublin for five years, graduating in 2016 with a major in electrical engineering. The last entry indicates he contemplated joining the Irish Defence Forces."

As we regroup, Jimmy sends Rosie out to get coffee and pastries before lighting into Basil. "He's a bumbling bureaucrat, doesn't know his ass from a hole in the ground. You'd think MI-6 would have information on its people of interest. But no, they don't even know where he was born!"

Rosie, just returning with a Dunkin Donuts bag, pipes up. "Gavin graduated from the U of Dublin and may have joined the Irish Army in 2016."

Jimmy looked at her with a little surprise.

Looking at Jimmy, I say, "Gavin was born at the Royal Victoria Hospital in 1993. His parents were Margaret and John Riddell. Both were killed by the time he was eleven." I then go into some detail outlining and describing my findings on Gavin's lineage. "His parents, grandparents, and great-grandparents were all advocates for the cause."

"So much for MI-6," said Danny. "We've found out that Gavin wants a united Ireland, most likely hates the English, is college educated, and may have military training. He has one brother whom he has little contact with, and we know of two possible living aunts. What am I missing?"

"Where is he?" says Rosie.

"Why is he here?" I add. "I'm not sure we can trust Basil's information that he's here to buy weapons. All our efforts in that direction have turned up nothing."

16 Dress Rehearsal

After the previous day's Basil bashing, we are still no closer to finding our targets, Gavin Riddell and his sidekick Billie Steele, a.k.a. Seamus O'Neil. We have found some background on Gavin. Born in 1993. Education, a college degree in electrical engineering. Parents dead, but two aunts are believed to be still with us as well as a twin brother, Hugh Riddell, a Dublin theater critic.

Hugh is advising Emerson College's School of Theater on a new play the school is sponsoring at the Cutler Majestic Theatre, The Ripe Turnip. The dress rehearsal is tonight.

"Rosie, are you ready for your debut?" I ask. "Carol and I will be there. Tell me about your role."

"Well, obviously, I'm not one of the Irish characters. I'm a flower girl, selling flowers from my cart. I sing the opening song. Later in the play, I have a duet with the lead actor. Damn, I'm nervous. I know I'm going to screw up."

"You are going to be fine. Just remember your namesake, Sister Tharpe. What would she do?"

"Steal the show," Rosie mumbles.

That evening Carol and I arrived at the theatre with Danny and Jimmy. Jimmy was so proud you'd think he was Rosie's father. Being an informal dress rehearsal, it was open seating.

As Carol was about to sit, she nudged me and said, "See the elderly couple over there," pointing with her eyes. "The couple with the lady in the wheelchair. They're the ones we had drinks with in Maine."

Looking closely, I agree and excuse Carol and myself from the Salt 'n Pepper contingent. We go to the other side of the auditorium and slip into the seats behind Bill and Trixie Hardy.

Carol, never the subtle one, taps Trixie on the shoulder, "Trixie, it's a surprise to see you here." Bill turns, "Sam, good to see you again; what brings you to the rehearsal?"

"Our receptionist is playing one of the major roles. She's the flower girl. And you?"

"Trixie's nephew is the play's adviser. It looks like the play is about to start. Do you and Carol have time for drinks afterward? We can get caught up."

Trixie's nephew. Which one is Trixie, Ellen or Grace?

During intermission, I leave Carol with the Hardys as I go to tell Danny I've found Bill Hardy and will be having drinks with him later.

The Ripe Turnip was a success. Rosie was terrific. I didn't realize what a great voice she had. Mabey, she didn't steal the show, but she captured the interest of a talent scout in the audience.

Bill suggested the lounge in the Ritz. It was just a block away. Being a member of the Ritz Club gave Bill access to the private lounge. We claimed some overstuffed chairs by the gas fireplace. Bill helped Trixie get situated in the chair next to Carol. The hostess took our orders. Bill had them charged to his room.

After a few minutes of idle talk, I asked Trixie if she knew Ellen O'Shaughnessy. Smiles faded, and quiet descended over our group.

Bill, somewhat defensively, "Who's that?"

Taking the bull by the horns, I say, "As I mention this summer, I'm a private investigator. We've been engaged by British authorities to locate potential IRA, or whatever the latest incarnation of that group is, terrorists looking to buy weapons. Gavin Riddell is Hugh Riddell's twin brother. Unless we've got it all wrong Trixie, Gavin is your nephew. Ellen O'Shaughnessy is one of Gavin's two aunts. This summer we met Gavin at The Bluebird Ocean Point Inn under his alias, Jimmy McKee. He and his partner were posing as a gay couple. We don't know his partner's name, but it's not Billie Steele, or Seamus O'Neil the name the Brits gave us."

Bill Hardy starts to get up, "We don't have to take these innuendos; please leave before I ask management to escort you out."

53

"Bill, back in the '90s you were a stanch IRA supporter. We've collected quite a folder of your pro-IRA articles. We've been working with the FBI to identify these terrorists. I'm meeting with Agent Bixby in the morning. I'd like to keep you and Trixie out of it, but you are giving me little choice."

He falls back into his chair. "You've done your homework. Let me fill in some gaps. Trixie's maiden name is Grace O'Shaughnessy. Ellen is her older sister. After the twin's mother was killed in 2004, Ellen and Grace took charge of Gavin and Hugh.

"I met Grace in 2006 while on assignment in Northern Ireland. At that time Gavin and Hugh were in their teens, associating with their father's former partners. They were following the father down the path of sectarian violence. One night there was a street confrontation with one of the orange militias. Ellen and Grace tried to extract the twins from the riot when Grace was shot in the back. She survived but lost the use of her legs.

"In the hospital, Ellen and I arrived at the same conclusion, the 'troubles' were not worth it for the family. Loved ones were either dead or in prison. The movement had obtained its main goal, an independent Ireland. Mabey not the whole of Ireland, but most of it. Ellen decided to move to Dublin with the twins, setting the cause aside. I would take Grace to New York for treatment, hoping she could regain the use of her legs. As the twins got older Hugh drifted into the arts, becoming a theater critic. Gavin, after graduating from the University of Dublin, returned to Belfast.

"We've had no contact with Gavin since he graduated. Then earlier this year he turns up in Maine with his buddy in a ridiculous disguise, posing as a gay couple.

"The evening you invited us to join you at the Carriage House, we were meeting later with Gavin. After a few drinks and catching up on our activities, he got to the point. He wanted some ideas on how to move some sensitive equipment, undetected, out of the country."

"Not weapons?" I asked.

"No! Some kind of electrical equipment," said Bill.

"I couldn't help him. All my old contacts, except one, were dead. The last I heard, Daniel Arms was in an upstate nursing home suffering from Alzheimer's.

54

"Trixie was arguing with Gavin to drop whatever he was up to. Not listening to her, he claimed to be on a mission to free his grandfather, Trixie's father, William O'Shaughnessy, and other high-value prisoners, from the max-security prison where they were being held.

"Billie, Seamus, or whatever his name is, was downright dismissive of Trixie. After a few heated words, I asked them to leave. We have not heard from them since then. And before you ask, I don't know where they are or how to contact them."

"You say he was planning on freeing his grandfather and others from prison. How?"

Looking at Trixie, Bill said "He didn't say. I'm guessing it may involve the equipment he wants to get out of the country."

17 MI-6 Recap

Monday morning, we were congratulating Rosie on her performance. "You did Sister Tharpe proud," I said. "Where did you learn to sing like that?"

"Growing up I was a choir member at the Church of the Holy Brotherhood. The choirmaster, an old man, and a hard taskmaster got results. He took me under his wing, telling me I had potential. He would have been proud last night."

Changing topics, Danny asks "How did your talk go with our friends the Hardy's."

"Well, they claim not to know where Gavin is or how to contact him. But here is the interesting twist. They claim Gavin is not looking for weapons, but for some electronic gear to be used in a prison break."

Danny and Jimmy stared at me. "Shit," says Jimmy. "Basil has had us going down rabbit holes when we should have focused on fox dens. I'm going to give that sorry excuse of an intelligent agent a piece of my mind."

Danny, holding up his hand, "He's the client, the paying client and I'll cut him some slack here. This is a curve ball for all of us. Sam, since you are the one that talked with Hardy, join me for a visit to the British Consulate this afternoon. I'll schedule time with Basil."

The British Consulate is relatively close to our office. Just a short walk across Longfellow Bridge. On the other hand, it was only two stops away on the MTA. The catch, the walk to the nearest MTA station was half the distance required to walk to the Consulate. It was a nice day; we decided on the twenty-minute walk.

We found Basil in the Consulate's cafeteria. He invited us to get some coffee, at our expense, and have a seat. We brought Basil up to date on Gavin's genealogy, on my talk with the Hardy's, and topped it off with our belief Gavin was not looking for weapons.

"A prison break you say," said the disbelieving Basil.

"His grandfather and other high-ranking IRA members are being held at HR Prison in Belfast. Why not? It would be a bigger public relations coup than a few smuggled weapons," I said.

Danny added, "Broaden your thinking. If a prison break is the objective, how could it be done? What can Gavin get here that is not available in the UK?

"Basil, we don't know where Gavin is; we've talked with his family members. We've run the weapons angel to ground, both acquisition and transportation. We think it is a dead end," said Danny, "I see three choices. One, we can continue wasting your money looking for weapons. Two, we can give you our final written report and terminate the case. Or three, investigate the plans for a prison break, specifically the means Gavin is looking for over here to carry it out."

Basil in his unruffled manner, sipping his tea, says "Let me talk with boys upstairs and I'll get back to you."

We decided to walk back to the office. It was a pleasant afternoon, as attested to by the activity on the Charles River. We stopped for a moment on the bridge to watch two eight-man shells having a mock race.

"I was on the crew team in high school," said Danny. "You row your heart out while a skinny coxswain keeps yelling at you 'pull harder' as he increases the tempo, directing the boat to the finish line. I'd like to say that's what Basil is doing, but I don't think he has a clue as to where the boat is headed."

Jimmy and Rosie remained in the office after Danny and I had left for the day, when Clifford Steele, Basil's shadow called. His message was "We want Gavin. Basil floated the thought that Gavin's objective was a prison break. Sir Reginald Longbottom, our Chief of Station, enjoyed the joke, noting the HR Prison in Belfast was one of the most secure facilities in the UK. But he senses Gavin is up to some mischief and asks that you continue looking for him."

Later when Jimmy passed on the message, he said with a grin "I recalled your words about them being a paying customer, so I refrained from providing my assessment of their intelligence capabilities."

18 MIT

It was a week later; I was sitting in The Coffee Shope listening to Lieutenant Doyle talk about his retirement plans. "Mind you, I have five more years, but it's not too late to plan. Janice and I have our eye on a cabin on the Merrimack River. Getting up in the morning, a pot of coffee, watching the river, and trying to decide, fishing or canoeing."

"You'd be bored stiff in a week," I said speaking from experience having retired from the BPD three years ago. "I've been there."

"Talking about boring," Doyle said, "Janice visited Dublin earlier this month with some of her theater friends. They read a review by one of the city's top critics, Hugh Riddell, about a new play. They had to see it."

"Hugh Riddell," I repeated. When was this review written?"

"Probably within the past month. Why?"

"Hugh Riddell is working with a theater group over at Emerson College. I recently met him. He's Gavin's twin brother ... you know, the guy we're looking for. Is Hugh jetting back and forth across the Atlantic or is Gavin impersonating Hugh?"

"Thanks," I said as I collected Maxie and headed back to Charles Street.

Reaching the top of the stairs, I found Rosie ensconced at her desk trying to look busy.

"Rosie, I have a task for you. Do an internet search for recent play reviews by Hugh Riddle. Focus on Dublin. Don't tell anyone in your theater group, but I think we have an impersonator."

I direct Maxie to her bed as I go into the inner office.

"I think we have an impersonator," I tell Jimmy. "and where is Danny, sleeping in late again?"

"He's following up on a lead one of his police contacts in Cambridge gave him. There may have been a sighting of Seamus O'Neil at one of the student night spots."

Before any comment on my part, Rosie was there with an excited look. "I found a theater review by Hugh Riddle in the Dublin Tattler. It was written three weeks ago."

"So?" Jimmy remarks.

"Three weeks ago, he was working with us here in Boston. Are there two theater critics named Hugh Riddle?" snaps Rosie.

"Okay, everyone, let's sit on this until Danny gets back."

It wasn't until midafternoon that Danny returned.

"Find anything of interest?" asks Jimmy.

"You're looking mighty pleased with yourself," Danny says, "but to answer your question, yes. Two bartenders at the Tombs, a popular student hangout, provided a tentative identification of Seamus, minus the mustache."

"Rosie, tell Danny what you found this morning."

As Danny is digesting Rosie's information, I start to outline a plan on the blackboard. I have three starting points: one, Gavin is in Boston impersonating his twin; two, the sighting of Seamus in Cambridge; and three, the Hardy's, lying their bloody little hearts out to me.

We review my initial assessment getting agreement. "How should we proceed?" I ask.

"We don't have the manpower I'd like," says Danny. I suggest we tail Gavin, a.k.a. Hugh. I think he's the brains and will lead us to Seamus. As for the Hardy's, save them for later when we have more information to confront them with."

Our first question is "Where is Gavin staying?" Next, asks Danny "Does he have any predictable schedule? Rosie, can you get answers to these two questions without drawing attention to yourself?"

Later in the day, Rosie calls in to report Gavin is staying at the Four Seasons Hotel on Boylston Street, across from the Boston

Common. She promises to have his schedule at Emerson in the morning.

Danny observes that Charles Street bisects the Common with the Four Seasons to the west and the College to the east and that there is on-street parking next to the Boston Common.

"Sam, how would you like to take Maxie for frequent walks on the Common? Based on the lay of the land, you could blend in with other dog walkers while monitoring Gavin's movements between Emerson and the hotel, detecting when he leaves the area. Either Jimmy or I will be available to tail him."

The next morning Rosie provides us with the theater group's schedule, the assumption being Gavin's schedule will be driven by the theater group's schedule. "That's a rather tenuous assumption," I observe.

Having no other options, we implement 'Observation Gavin.'

During this time Gavin pretty much adhered to the Emerson theater group's schedule. Deviations took him to local bookstores, shopping at Macy's, formerly Filene's, and lunch at Durgan Park. All this while one young lady, with two miniature poodles, was starting to make moves on me.

On the fourth day, Gavin made an unexpected move. He left Emerson midmorning, flagged a taxi, and headed north up Charles Street. My SUV was parked fifty feet away on Charles Street. I ran to it, and not having time to load Maxie in the back, she got to ride shotgun with her head out the window.

Traffic was moderately heavy. The taxi was three cars ahead. I was on the phone with Danny as I passed Abe's Bookstore. "I think he's headed to Longfellow Bridge, maybe going to Cambridge. I could use a little backup here."

"On my way! Don't lose him," said an excited Danny. "Stay on the line."

I follow the taxi across the bridge. On the far side, he turns off the main thoroughfare, heading toward the Massachusetts Institute of Technology complex. "Danny, Gavin's getting out of the taxi on Vassar Street by the College of Computing. I've pulled over into a construction zone; still have eyes on him. He's crossing the street;

looks like he's headed to the MIT Research Laboratory of Electronics."

"I've just parked in the parking garage," Danny says as he taps on my window.

"That building over there," I point. "You're thirty seconds behind him." He hurries across the street, disappearing into the front entrance. I entered back into traffic and a block later found a place to park. Maxie and I then proceeded to walk back the way we came.

"Danny, Maxie and I are on the street. Can't stay long without drawing attention. Anything I can do?"

"Walk down the street and back. Give me five minutes."

On my way back Gavin and a 'teenager' exited the Research Laboratory of Electronics building; headed back to where I initially parked. Danny, a few paces behind. "Sam, pull your car over to the next block, I think I heard them say something about lunch."

The two end up in a cafe, Café Luna, which is not far from the married student housing area where I find a place to park. Good view of the cafe. Danny's tapping on my window and as he opens the passenger door, asks me to put Maxie in the back seat. "That was close in there. He walked by me, but I don't think he noticed me. We may be here awhile," he says, "got any nut bars?"

Forty-five minutes later the two leave the cafe, looking well-fed. Gavin flags down a taxi. "Okay Sam, you got the taxi, I'm going to follow Gavin's friend," and Danny is out of the SUV.

The taxi returns Gavin to Emerson with no side trips and no excitement.

19 Sammy

Late that day Jimmy picks up the 'Gavin watch.' He's at Emmerson College under the pretext of talking with Rosie. Between the two of them, they stick with Gavin when he goes back to his hotel.

A short time later he's on the move again, landing at Maggiano's, a noted Italian restaurant, where he meets two men and a woman. Rosie and Jimmy take a table on the far side of the room. "It's looking like Gavin will be here for a while so let's order dinner," says Jimmy.

"I've always wanted to eat here but was intimidated by its ambiance. It looks kinda like a place the 'Godfather' would hold court."

"Management has done a good job on that front," said Jimmy, "but Maggiano's is a chain. The food is good though. I recommend the Chicken Parmesan."

Pulling out his phone Jimmy says, "I'm going to wander across the room and try to get some photos of the three with Gavin. Hopefully, he won't notice me. After a quick cruise around the room, Jimmy is back.

"They were so engrossed in their conversation the Pope could have walked in and they wouldn't have noticed."

Scrolling through the pictures just taken, Jimmy selects two. "These are pretty good," he says showing them to Rosie. "Wonder who they are? Have they ever been around the theater?" he asks her.

"No."

I'll send them to Danny, and I think I'll also send them to Doyle to see if they are in the BPD's database.

The rest of the evening was mostly uneventful. As Jimmy and Rosie were leaving, following the Gavin party, Gavin caught sight of Rosie and congratulated her on her dress rehearsal performance.

The following morning it was decided to suspend 'Observation Gavin' for a few days. They were concerned they had gotten too close at Maggiano's. No need to spook him if it could be avoided.

"Those are interesting photos, Jimmy. Any idea who they are?" asked Danny.

"No. I sent them to Doyle to see if he gets a hit but it's too early to expect a callback. Just spit-balling here, but do you think MI-6 might have a handle on them? I'll give Basil a call when we're done here."

"Sam and I had an interesting day yesterday," said Danny. Followed Gavin to MIT where he had lunch with one of the faculty, Dr. John Kaminski."

"Faculty, Doctor ... that teenager?" sputters Sam.

"Yup," said Danny, "one of MIT's youngest faculty members. Dr. Kaminski is a noted scientist, working on the cutting edge of electronic innovations."

"When I followed him back to the research center, he was in the elevator with the doors shutting before I could catch him. But it turned out the lobby guard is a retired police sergeant I worked with years ago. Kaminski's laboratory is on the third floor. The area is restricted; Kaminski is working on a sensitive government grant. The only people allowed in the area are a few MIT bigwigs, a supervised cleaning crew, and his assistant, Simphiwe Mashatile, nicknamed Sammy. Sammy is a graduate student from South Africa, here under a student exchange program."

"Jimmy, I think you should be the one to approach Sammy. You're black, he's black. I don't know if he has any racial hangups so let's not spook him," said Danny.

"Okay but let me call Basil first," said Jimmy.

Jimmy's call to Basil resulted in some excitement. Jimmy emailed Basil the two selected photos. Before I could refill my coffee mug, Basil was on the speaker phone. "Where did you get these pictures?" he's demanding.

"Why, who are they," Jimmy fires back.

Losing some steam, Basil answers, "They are minor board members of The Irish Cultural Centre. The Center's mission is to preserve and promote Irish culture and heritage through music, dance, arts, and history. But they've also led recent protests supporting the unification of Ireland. It's our best guess, it's the latter that has Gavin talking with them."

Listening to this exchange, Danny decides to spend the day at the Cultural Center to see what can be learned about the three in the photo.

"And I'll call it a day and go back to the Common to flirt with the poodle lady," I said.

Late in the afternoon, Jimmy is on the MIT campus tracking Sammy. It turns out Sammy has a place at 'The Lofts of Kendall Square,' on Binney Street. It's several blocks from the campus which gave Jimmy a challenge following Sammy on foot without being detected.

Sammy's unit was on the corner of the complex and across the street from a Chinese restaurant. Jimmy finds a window seat. "Damn, I'm tired of Chinese food," Jimmy says to himself. Two hours later as the restaurant owner is getting ready to ask Jimmy to move on, Sammy emerges dressed in his 'going out to party' clothes.

Still on foot, Sammy heads three blocks over to the area known as 'The Port' which is mostly residential but is a growing part of Cambridge's diversity scene with its cluster of low-key pubs, cocktail bars, and trendy late-night eateries. Once there Sammy goes into the student hangout Danny mentioned earlier, The Tombs. From a perch at the far end of the bar, Jimmy has eyes on Sammy who is bantering with, what appears to be, a group of students. As the students drift off Jimmy moves up the bar, to a seat or two away from Sammy.

Turning toward Jimmy, Sammy says, "You've been following me for several hours now. Who are you and what do you want?"

Surprised and embarrassed that he has been discovered, Jimmy responds "Do you know Seamus O'Neil?"

"Why?"

"He's a terrorist and we want to know what he is up to."

Before Sammy could ask who the 'we' were, Seamus walks up and asks Sammy, "Who's your friend?"

"A brother from back home. He's still trying to learn the language. American English is a bitch. What can I order for you?"

65

"A short pint. I'm meeting my partner up the street in twenty minutes. If you are still interested, I'll be back in an hour or so."

The bartender, a young woman, probably a student, sets a half pint in front of Seamus. He thanks her, drains it, and is out the door.

Sammy turned back to me. "You look like a cop," he says.

Jimmy, still trying to get his head around what just happened, takes a minute or two to respond. "I'm a private investigator. We, my partner and I, have been engaged to find out what O'Neil and his people are up to. They have ties to the IRA."

"I sympathize with the IRA," says Sammy. "British colonialism oppressed my ancestors, took their land. Made us, their sons and daughters, redundant in our own country."

"And my people were enslaved, worked the white man's plantations," said Jimmy, "but that was then. We need to move forward. But working with terrorists is not the way to go. From what I can see, you are doing pretty well for yourself. You have a nice gig as an exchange student and a bright future. Working with O'Neil will not work out well for you. He's being tracked by the FBI and MI-6. He and his associates are going down."

"Now that my cover has been blown, I can be reached at this number," Jimmy says as he writes his cell number on a napkin. "I think we can help each other."

20 A Plan Emerges

The three PIs were in the office the next day. Given it was a Saturday, this was unusual.

Jimmy, embarrassed his cover was busted by Sammy, told of his encounter with Sammy and the overheard conversation between Sammy and Seamus. "We should have had someone on Gavin last night, I bet Seamus was meeting Gavin after he left Sammy. I left my number with Sammy, and late last night he called. Said he'd like to meet with me and my partner to discuss the offer Seamus made him."

Danny had had little luck at the Irish Cultural Center. The three people he was looking for were prominent board members. The only one in was Elizabeth Borden. "I was able to strike up a conversation with her under the pretext of havening seen her the night before at Maggiano's where I was having dinner with my daughter. We were celebrating her recent academic achievements. Elizabeth insisted on being called Lizzie. She acknowledged she was there, having dinner with a friend from the 'old' country. I didn't press it, but I think we might have a link between her and Gavin."

"And how did your day go Sam? Danny asks.

"Oh, the poodle lady asked me out on a date. It went downhill when I told her I'd have to check with my wife."

Looking over at the desk, Jimmy saw the light blinking on the answering machine. It was a call from Doyle, late yesterday. "Jimmy, got your photos. The three people you are asking about are with The Irish Cultural Centre. They surface every March protesting for a unified Ireland. This year's St. Patty's Day march got out of hand; the three were jailed for disorderly conduct. There are also allegations that these three are tied to The Provisionals in Northern Ireland.

"I'm going to call Sammy and see if I can meet with him today. Danny?"

"Call him," said Danny, I'm free all day. Sam, go spend the day with Carol … don't want her getting jealous over the poodle lady."

Sammy was available and said he'd meet them at two at the Shy Bird Restaurant, inside.

Danny did a quick Google search to locate the restaurant, "Well look at this," he said. "The Shy Bird is next door to the British General Counsel's offices."

Parking was always a bear in Cambridge, and it was worse on the weekends. The two decided to walk. Most restaurant patrons were enjoying patio seating. It was obvious Sammy did not want to be seen with PIs. He was at a table in the far interior of the restaurant.

Jimmy took the lead in talking with Sammy. He introduced Danny and explained they were both former cops, retired, and were now the Salt 'n Pepper Detective Agency.

"Salt 'n Pepper?" said Sammy.

Danny responded, "When we were with the Boston Police Department, we were a team for many years. We were given the nickname Salt 'n Pepper for obvious reasons."

Sammy picking up the conversation, "Thinking about your comments yesterday, that the FBI and MI-6 were watching Seamus, I have to agree, he is not my best bet for my future."

"What's his interest in you?" Jimmy asks.

"I am Dr. Kaminski's graduate intern. Kaminski has developed a new technology that allows one to take over an electrical grid. Seamus wants it, or at least a working model that can be used in a limited setting."

"Kaminski has a working model?"

"Almost, but it needs a few tweaks.

"Just what does this device do?" asks Danny.

"That's the neat part. It searches the grid in the immediate area, detects backup generators, disables them, and then disables the substation. With that device, I could shut down the school and the rest of Cambridge wouldn't be affected."

"That must be a big piece of equipment," said Jimmy.

"No, no bigger than a large suitcase."

Danny looks at Jimmy, "Prison Break?"

"And what does Seamus want, you to steal it?" Danny says looking at Sammy.

"Yes."

Over the next several days, coordinating with the BPD and FBI, a plan emerges. Doyle and Bixby will help Sammy steal the device. Danny tells Basil of the emerging plan. MI-6's buy-in is critical to the success of the plan.

Agent Bixby along with Danny visits Dr. Kaminski where Danny provides the doctor with the background of the case. He starts his story, by telling of the Brits contracting Salt 'n Pepper to track IRA terrorists.

"Initially it was thought they were looking to smuggle weapons to Northern Ireland. But it now appears they are interested in your work.

"You met with an Irishman three days ago. Can you tell us about him?" Danny asks.

"What, you mean Michael Collins? He claims to be an old acquaintance that I met at the University of Dublin, almost a decade ago when I was doing some graduate work. He called out of the blue last week asking to get together. I didn't remember him, and the face and name were a puzzle. We had lunch, shared some common memories and that was that."

"That was Gavin Riddell, and he did attend the University of Dublin," said Danny. "Anything else?"

"Well, yes. In hindsight, he seemed overly curious about my current work. It felt like he was angling to be invited to visit my laboratory. I had to explain it was a restricted area.

"We identified Gavin Riddell and Seamus O'Neil. Seamus's role is to obtain a working model of your invention. He plans to have Sammy help steal it. Sammy by the way spilled the beans and is working with us."

"Gavin's role is to move your working model out of the country. I think, but there is some disagreement here, that The Irish Cultural Centre will be key in moving the equipment."

Agent Bixby picks it up. "We know you are working under a government grant and your work is classified. What we are proposing is a rather audacious plan that needs your support. You will be fully indemnified by the government if you participate." Joyce then goes on to outline the emerging plan.

A day later Basil is at the Salt 'n Pepper office. Danny lays out the plan that was put into play by Joyce, Doyle, and Dr. Kaminski. Basil is soon smiling.

"We don't know if Hugh Riddell is part of this, but we suggest you put him under surveillance. If I were to bet," said Danny, "I'd say he is one of the key players on your side of the Atlantic."

21 Theft

Gavin and Seamus had a plan. Sammy, who was now working for the FBI, was a key part of that plan. Their plan:

They would strike late Friday night when students were roaming the streets looking for the next party. Sammy's task was to access Dr. Kaminski's lab, pack up the prototype in the large suitcase Gavin provided and exit the Research Laboratory of Electronics with the suitcase.

Seamus's role was to create a diversion so Sammy could walk out undetected and take the suitcase across the street to be hidden in a construction storage locker. Gavin would collect it later that weekend. The chance of the construction crew working that weekend, or any weekend, was nil. After all, they were unionized city employees.

An Uber ride would be arranged to collect Sammy and whisk him away.

Gavin would have a ride outside for Seamus's escape.

That was the plan. What went down was a bit different.

Sammy was challenged when he entered the building. The guard wanted to know why he was there so late. After a bullshit reason was given, the guard let him in, but he was now suspicious.

The suitcase, although big enough, had the wrong dimensions; it was not wide enough. Sammy had to improvise using an electric cord to tie the suitcase shut, leaving a four-inch gap.

On his cell, he called Seamus when he was about to get out of the elevator. Gavin threw a 'flash bang' into the lobby to disable the guard. _Unfortunately, the guard was around the corner in the hallway returning from the restroom. He was not disabled and when Sammy appeared from the smoke with the suspicious suitcase, he pulled his sidearm ordering him down. As this happened, Seamus entered the lobby, saw the problem, and shot the guard, killing him._

The two rushed out of the building, Seamus throwing a second flash bang to distract the crowd, crossed the street to Sammy's waiting Uber ride. They stashed the suitcase in the equipment storage unit as planned and the two departed. The driver became somewhat agitated when Seamus put his gun to the driver's head, and distracted, drove into a city bus, head-on. Seamus shot him in the head as the two made their escape on foot into Cambridge's back streets. By this time Sammy was a basket case. Gavin found them hiding in an ally. They all went to the rental on the west side of Cambridge where Seamus was staying.

Sunday morning the three returned to retrieve the suitcase. It was where Sammy had stashed it. As Gavin was placing the suitcase in the car trunk, Seamus shot Sammy, cleaning up possible loose ends. The two sped off into the Sunday morning traffic.

A guard in an adjacent building thought he heard a gunshot, and after Friday night's excitement, had a drawn weapon as he got to the sidewalk. He saw a late model car, two intersections down the street, making a hasty getaway. Looking around he saw a body in the construction area. The man was still alive. He applied pressure to the wound and called 911. The paramedics were able to stabilize Sammy on the way to the hospital.

Early Monday morning Gavin was at the loading dock of the Irish Cultural Center's auditorium where he met Lizzie. He retrieved the suitcase from the Amazon delivery truck he had hijacked in the very early morning hours.

The Cultural Center hosted a special performance by 'Dublin's Prancing Lasses' over the weekend. It was the last stop on the group's tour of the States. Work had started Sunday evening to pack the group's equipment. Lizzie and Gavin quickly opened one of the containers and made room for the suitcase. With a few nails, Gavin had the container resealed.

By early that afternoon the 'Dublin's Prancing Lasses' equipment was in the belly of a Ryanair cargo jet, three hundred miles east of Boston.

22 Effects

"That was a royal f...k up!" said Doyle. "Two dead and one in the hospital."

"I think it's time we brought Basil into this," said Bixby. "The BPD has issued an arrest warrant for Seamus and Gavin warning that they are armed and dangerous. We have alerted all our field offices in the Northeast to be on the lookout for them."

It was midday Monday as I sat with Danny and Joyce recapping the weekend events. I reported Gavin was nowhere to be found. He had vacated the Four Seasons Hotel and had skipped weekend rehearsals at Emmerson. We had no idea where Seamus had been staying but were willing to bet, he was not there now.

Lieutenant Doyle's men were assigned to monitor the Irish Cultural Center. There was some activity at the Center early Monday, but nothing that warranted intervention, only an Amazon delivery truck. Midmorning there was a box truck collecting the 'Dublin's Prancing Lasses' crated musical instruments and other paraphernalia for shipment back to Dublin. With no search warrant, all the team could do was watch.

Jimmy was just returning from the hospital and reported Sammy would make a full recovery. If not for the security guard's quick action, Sammy would be dead. "He's really worried about being charged as an accomplice to murder," Jimmy said. Looking at Joyce, "I assured him that would not happen; he'd probably come out of this as a hero."

Danny agreed with Joyce and placed a call to Basil Montgomery telling the receptionist he needed to talk with Basil. "He's not available," she answered.

Disconnecting Danny says, "That's great; Basil and Sir Reginald are unavailable; they're playing golf at the 'Presidents Golf Course' in Quincy."

Joyce made a quick call, a few muffled words, she invited us to the roof of the FBI building. As we opened the door to the roof, an FBI helicopter was setting down. "Our ride," she said.

While en route, a call to the golf course located the party of interest. Joyce directed the pilot to set down by the 14th Tee where we disrupted Sir Regie who was just teeing off sending his ball into the woods.

Danny introduced Agent Bixby, emphasizing FBI, to the foursome and asked if we could have a private word with Sir Reginald Longbottom and Mr. Basil Montgomery.

Danny recapped the weekend's events. "Your boys have been quite busy Basil. Three shootings, two deaths. Classified equipment stolen from MIT. We think this equipment is intended to facilitate the prison break we mentioned earlier."

Bixby picks it up, "Given we don't know where the equipment is, or where Gavin and Seamus are, we are suggesting you heighten security at the HR Prison."

At which point Sir Reginald Longbottom puffed his chest and said, "The Belfast HR Prison is the most secure prison in the UK," walked back to the tee box, and teed up a replacement ball.

As we boarded the helicopter Danny pulls Basil aside, "We need to talk. Soon!"

23 Dublin

Meanwhile, in Dublin Hugh Riddell and his buddy Connor slipped into The Emerald Theater, home of the Prancing Lasses, just after the air freight delivery truck left the loading dock. They located the crate with the suitcase, popped the crate open, and departed with the suitcase in Connor's Vauxhall.

They headed north to Dundalk just south of Belfast but still in the Republic of Ireland. The IRLA commandeered a deserted farmhouse on the outskirts of the town where they were staging men and equipment for the pending prison break.

As long as the European Union and the United Kingdom continued to spare over BREXIT borders, there was no checkpoint between the two countries, just an open road, the A1. The plan that emerged had Hugh and Connor taking Kaminski's apparatus to Maghaberry, the village abutting the prison. A small house in the village had been leased. This is where the apparatus would be tied into the grid. There is a large solar farm on the east side of the prison with a service road going through the field of panels leading to a service entrance to the prison. The main prison facility is on the immediate interior of the inner wall.

At seven in the morning, when the inmates were in the dining area of the main facility, IRLA soldiers would storm the back gate, and using explosives, breach the interior wall.

William O'Shaughnessy, a senior leader in The Provisionals, and Hugh's maternal grandfather, was in on the plan. As the explosives detonated, he and his men would initiate a prison riot to break out of *the main prison facility, going to the backside where the IRLA would have escape vehicles waiting on the other side of the breached wall.*

At seven a.m. sharp Hugh would engage Kaminski's machine, blacking out the immediate area. Without electricity communications would be disrupted, gates would not operate, and alarm systems would be down. If Kaminski's apparatus works as advertised, backup generators would not kick in.

What actually happened differed. Basil's heads up to the Gardai, the national police service of Ireland, placed Hugh under observation before the Ryanair cargo jet landed at Dublin's International Airport. An IRLA informant notified the Gardai of the Dundalk staging area. On the Union Jack side, appropriate MI-5 departments were alerted.

On the morning of the prison break, Hugh's attempt to energize Kaminski's machine resulted in an explosion, taking half his face. The electric grid remained fully energized, and the IRLA's assault team was decimated as they emerged from the solar field to attack the prison's back gate.

William O'Shaughnessy's aborted prison riot got him thirty days in solitary.

Other than the IRLA and the prisoners, all were happy. Well, not all. Climate change activists were enraged by the damage caused by the gunfire to a significant number of solar panels.

24 Maine

Doyle invites, perhaps invite is too weak a word, Danny, Jimmy, and me to The Coffee Shope to discuss our case. Ever since the murders, the BPD has had an all-points bulletin for Gavin and Seamus. There have been no sightings.

"The Chief is all over my ass," says Doyle. "Earlier I briefed him on our plan, now he's laying these killings at my feet. He wants Gavin and Seamus. We've asked the NYPD to monitor the Hardys' penthouse in case they show up there. The NYPD reported back that the Hardys are out of town. Any ideas where else we should be looking?"

As we sit looking at each other, an idea comes to mind. I pulled out my cell phone and call The Bluebird Ocean Point Inn in Maine. "Hello, this is Sam Goodman. My wife and I stayed with you earlier this year. Yes, we enjoyed our stay and plan to return. That's the reason for this call. When we were there, we met an Irish couple, Jimmy McKee, and his wife Billie Steele. They mentioned they'd probably be there again later this year ... they are there now. Great. Would you reserve a cabin for my wife and me, we'll be up tomorrow ... no, please don't tell them; we want to surprise them. Thank you."

"Okay, I found them," I said. "I'll bet you dollars to donuts that the Hardys are at their Ocean Point cottage."

"Good work said," Doyle. "I'll call the Maine State Police and have them picked up."

"Can you hold off on that," said Danny. I'd like to be there. And I would like to also get the Hardys."

"There is only one road on the peninsula going out to the tip," I said. "Can the locals monitor that road until we get there? We can be there, midday tomorrow,".

"Jesus," said Danny. "The Chief will have my nuts if they get away. I'll notify the State Police that two wanted men, wanted for murder, are holed up on Linekin Neck and ask that they monitor the access road until you get there."

"Let's move it, Danny. I'm Driving. Go get your gear and I'll meet you at the office in 30. Jimmy, you with us?"

"No, I'll stay here and coordinate with Bixby and Basil."

Twenty minutes later I'm parked in front of Abe's Bookstore. Danny's waiting at the curb with a small duffle bag. Guns? Clothes?

He hops into the passenger's seat and looks back, "I see you brought back up," he says as Maxie raises her head in the back of the SUV, wagging her tail.

It's midafternoon when we leave Boston. Switching drivers, we covered the two hundred-plus miles to Bangor in less than four hours. We found the State Police Barracks and checked in with the duty officer, Corporal Watkins, identifying ourselves.

"You got here fast," the Corporal said with a grin. "Captain Smith is expecting you ... in the morning. He's at home; I'll call him now. Doyle didn't say you'd be riding the rocket express."

After a quick discussion with Smith, Danny says, "We'll get a quick nap, in one of the cells, warming it up for Seamus and Gavin. Smith said we'll tackle The Bluebird Ocean Point Inn at about four tomorrow morning. We can be there, but the State Police will be the ones to take them down."

I hardly shut my eyes when Watkins is waking us, from a distance. Maxie is up, growling, and watching him. "That dog scares me," he said. "The teams forming up now, out front."

I think most of the men assigned to the Bangor State Police Barracks were there; three police cruisers and two decked-out SUVs.

"This is the most excitement my men have had for a while," said Captain Smith. "We had a missing family last year. They got stranded on one of the logging roads when their car broke down. You two take up the rear position ... and stay out of the way."

It was close to four-thirty when we arrived at the Inn. The Inn's owner and the Captain were lodge brothers. Late last night they had a short talk placing the duo in the cabin on the far side of the complex.

The cabin of interest was nestled in the pines, accessible from only two sides. Two vehicles, one cruiser and my SUV were held back in the Inn's parking lot. At five sharp flash bangs flew and spotlights illuminated. Bullhorns called for the two to surrender. As Gavin stumbled out onto the cabin's porch, Seamus burst out the back door, shot one of the troopers in the containment perimeter, and fled into the woods.

Seeing Seamus's escape, I released Maxie and set off in pursuit. Danny told Captain Smith what I was doing and asked that he order his men down ... he didn't want any stray rounds hitting me.

There was very little light this early in the dawn as I raced through the woods, branches slapping my face. My flashlight provided minimal help. I was following Maxie. In five minutes, maybe less, she had Seamus on the ground chewing his arm. The flashlight lit up his pistol which was knocked from his hand when eighty pounds of German Shepherd descended on him.

Three troopers followed me into the woods. When they arrived, they said, "When your dog is done, we'll cuff him?"

We stumbled out of the woods, Gavin in cuffs between the two biggest troopers. Captain Smith was watching.

"I thought I told you to stay on the sideline?" the Captain said. "Fortunately, as your friend here said, you're proactive. Thank you and your dog for your assistance."

25 Aftermath

"We have one more stop," Danny told Captain Smith. "Bill and Trixie Hardy, they have a cottage out on the point. We can't tie them to a specific crime but at a minimum, we know they are accessories to theft, murder, and harboring fugitives. And to top it off, they lied to us. There is no warrant out for them so there is nothing you can do. But once you get things wrapped up here, if you could just follow us to their cottage and ..."

The sun is just coming up. I remember Bill saying he likes to be out early walking Emelie, their basset hound.

Two police cruisers, lights flashing, followed Danny and me out the Shore Road to the Ocean Point community. We found Bill on the ocean side of the road. I have his attention. "Bill if you could spare me a minute, I think we should go inside and talk." I wave and the two cruisers drive off. "They'll be back if I call them. And do you mind if my partner joins us?"

Once inside seated in their living room, Trixie emerges in her bathrobe. Coffee is not offered.

Looking at them I say, "Bill, you lied to me. You knew Gavin was impersonating Hugh. Is Hugh part of this?

"You also knew what they were up to, but we can't tie you to it. You are also guilty of protecting fleeing fugitives. Again, we can't prove that."

As I'm berating the Hardys Danny is on his cell. "Sam, I have Basil on the line. He has an interesting story. Should I put him on the phone's speaker?

"Yes, I'm curious to hear what he has to report."

"Sam good morning. I understand the Hardys are listening. We had some excitement in Belfast this morning. As your team predicted, Hugh Riddell intercepted the Prancing Lasses' shipment back to Dublin and retrieved the suitcase Gavin had hidden in it. We were a bit surprised when he and his partner left for Belfast. The prison break was on a fast track. We're guessing they were concerned news of the MIT theft may be tied to them.

"This morning when the prisoners in HR Prison were in the dining hall, the IRLA launched their attack, and were decimated.

"Concurrent with the attack, Hugh attempted to disrupt electrical power to the prison complex using Dr. Kaminski's electric grid disrupter that you folks allowed to be stolen. It blew up when engaged. Hugh lost half his face.

"Working with the Republic of Ireland's authorities, we captured or identified most of the active IRLA members. Teams have been sent to arrest the latter.

"We are saddened by the loss of American life due to Gavin. We will be working with the State Department to make restitution to their families."

As Danny disconnected, I turned to Trixie, "Has sectarian violence been worth the costs to your family? Parents and siblings dead. Nephews in prison, one disfigured for life. We may not be able to charge either of you, but this failure will remain with you for the rest of your life."

***

The following week the Chief of the Boston Police Department invited Doyle in for a debriefing. The Chief was miffed that MI-6 was getting all the press regarding the takedown of the IRA terrorist ring. The Chief downplayed the FBI's role, "They are always riding on the back of others for good press," he said, "and as for the Salt n' Pepper team, nothing less would be expected of our former officers."

END

Made in the USA
Middletown, DE
23 October 2023